"RIDE HIM DOWN!"

The voice came out of the fire-haunted darkness and then horses came thundering out of a furnace of black and yellow smoke . . .

Lansen cursed the shapeless figures shrouded by smoke. He sprawled on the ground. The earth scored his chest and shoulders.

And then again he heard the voice.

"RIDE HIM DOWN!"

SHOWDOWN
AT GILA BEND

Kingsley West

WILDSIDE PRESS

CHAPTER ONE

LATIGO Lansen backed away and filled his lungs. Blood from the arm wound dripped on the ground. He stared at the body of the Apache. His legs hurt and trembled. "No, sir!" he shouted in tremendous relief. "Nobody's killing me!"

The gelding watched and came close. Latigo walked from the dead Indian to the stream, stripped off the shirt, washed his chest and shoulders and bathed the stab wound. Wind came back and fluttered the feather in the red man's hair. He didn't bury the Indian and the sky turned copper and black before he slept. Tomorrow had better be good.

His name was Lat, which was short for Latimer Lansen, but nobody ever called him that. Latigo was the name that stuck to him like a burr and suited him well. He was twenty-six years old, tall and straight-backed in the saddle, with a flat stringy body that needed a solid month of woman's cooking. His belly was lean and liked cold water. Long legs reached from narrow hips that were easy on a saddle and his hands knew their way about a horse or a gun. Close to his knee in the saddle holster hung a Winchester model 1866, well used and all the better for that.

He crossed the wide hardpan flat behind the ranchhouse and reined. He leaned hands on horn and cantle and twisted in the saddle. There were no cattle anywhere, no noise, no blue smoke climbing from the chimney, the air curious and silent.

In front of the house waited two wagons and a buckboard loaded and ready to move. Two lighter squawhitched riding horses stood by the tail of the buckboard. The door of the house stood open and as Latigo rode close a man came out carrying a gunnysack bundle, then a young fellow followed by a woman.

The man was tall and straight and brown-faced with a grey moustache and walked boldly. Latigo touched the brim of his hat. All three hesitated and then came on. The woman and the boy nodded greetings but the man's face did not change much.

"Mind if I water my horse?"

The man nodded permission and the boy pointed with the gunnysack pack he carried. "Sure. Find all the water you want over there."

"Thanks. You mind if I get down? Been riding a long time."

The man moved his head. His expression lost edge; hesitation left his eyes. "Sure, son. Get off your horse. Not every day we see strangers that are welcome."

Latigo led the gelding to water and walked back. The man waited for him and the woman and the boy stood by the buckboard. He touched his hat again to the woman. " 'Day, ma'am," he said.

She packed the gunnysack bundle into place. "Haven't a thing to offer, neighbour," she said, eyes troubled but brave. "Right sorry about it, seeing you're a stranger and all."

"Nothing left in the house at all," added the boy.

"Wasn't hoping for food, ma'am," said Latigo. "Had coffee a little while ago."

The older man's face was friendly enough, trouble on his mind and signs of worry on his forehead. The boy looked eighteen, all bone, strong as an ox and six feet tall, as good to look at as a good new day. Latigo reckoned he was the son. "You folks moving?" he asked.

The man nodded. The woman's lips puckered and her eyes moved away. The boy bristled with anger. His hands clenched. He glared at his father. The man breathed deeply but the boy was ready to talk. "Yes, mister," he said. "That's what we're doing ... moving!"

The father spoke quietly. "That's no way to talk, son," he said. "I don't want to hear that kind of talk. What we're doing is best for all of us."

The boy's eyes blazed. Yellow hair fell across his forehead. He glared at Latigo, then at his father. "Aren't you angry, Pa?" he demanded. "Aren't you real honest-to-God spitting mad?" He waited seconds. There was no answer. Straight as a pine tree, he turned to Latigo. "Wouldn't you be, mister, if it was you?"

Latigo looked from the father to the angry youth. "I

6

don't know what's happening," he said. "I'm a stranger."

The man worked roughly at the gunnysack bundles behind the seat of the buckboard. "I don't want to hear any more of that kind of talk, son," he said. "I told you. Now let it be!" He strode towards the house and slowed after five paces.

"We're running away, Pa!" cried the boy. "That's what we're doing. We're letting them run us off our own land!"

The man stopped walking. Latigo turned in time to see pride leave the rancher's shoulders and his hands tighten. The man turned and sighed deeply, brown face lighted by sunshine.

The boy's eyes brightened. "Pa, I'm on your side," he said loudly, earnestly, face creased and finely chiselled. "I'll do anything you say, anything at all. I'll go if I have to but, Pa, I don't want to run away!" His eyes never left his father's face and his hands pleaded. The woman began to cry a little. She turned to the buckboard and rested forehead on hand.

"If you folks are in trouble I'm sorry I butted in," said Latigo. "You want me to, I'll go."

"No," said the father. "It's none of your doing. Ma is sorry she can't be hospitable but," he paused and breathed and looked at the loaded wagons, "as you can see, mister, we're leaving."

"We don't have to, Pa," said the youth.

The man's eyes burned with anger he did not feel. "It's the only thing I can do, son!" he said sharply, hurt because he had to say it and because the boy was his son.

The youth moved and stood before Latigo. "Mister, will you stay for a minute? Will you listen if I tell you?"

"Do anything I can," said Latigo.

"There, Pa, there! You hear what the man says!"

"It's none of his business, son!"

The boy was quick. He held Latigo's arm and addressed his father. "Let me tell him, Pa. Just so he'll know!"

The woman turned from the side of the buckboard. "Let the boy speak, Andrew. He's got a right . . ."

"Thanks, Ma," said the youth and waited for a sign from his father.

The older man regarded Latigo. "You're a stranger, mister. I guess there's no harm in telling you."

7

The woman was quiet, waiting. The boy's eyes stayed on Latigo. The father did the telling. "I'm Andrew Hemingway," he said. "This here is my wife, Emily, and this is Buck, my boy. He's eighteen years old. That's why I'm doing what I am." He walked from the wagon to the fence of an empty corral. Latigo and the boy followed. "Nearly all you can see was my land. All that range ahead of you, right down to the big arroyo. You can't see it but it's there." He turned and pointed to the house. "Then out to the butte. From there east to where my marker is set up. South of us there's wooded country and a creek that runs into the Gila river..." Latigo listened. The rancher described his land and its edges, a big comfortable spread, unfenced and with plenty of water. The house was stone built but the barn to the side had been burned down. "We're close enough to the river for it all to be good land, mister. It's got twenty years of my life in it. But, like Buck says, we're running away."

Latigo asked the question the rancher waited to hear. "Why?"

The boy stared at the ground in shame, eyes burning at what his father would say. "We're being driven out," said Hemingway. Latigo looked over the rancher's shoulder at the charred uprights of the barn. "Seven or eight years ago Matthew Kincaid came here. He was a cattleman same as the rest of us. We didn't think anything was wrong until it was too late. He started buying up all the land. Then he brought in hired guns. If he couldn't buy your land peaceable, he made you glad to sell. They drove off my beef cattle. They spoiled my water so my cattle died. They burned down my barn. Soon I couldn't get anybody to work for me. Two of my cowhands were killed. I buried them down by the stream." He paused, breathed deeply and lowered his shoulders, eyes avoiding his son, pride of living and fearlessness gone out of him. "I can't fight back, mister. Too old to learn how. Been a peaceable man too long for that. Buck here would fight. He's young, he wants to fight, but he's all I've got so I won't let him fight. Got his mother to think about."

"So you're selling to Kincaid?"

Hemingway nodded. "Nothing else for me to do. Not enough ranchers left in Gila valley to fight back. He went at us one at a time."

8

"Isn't there a sheriff in Gila Bend?"

"Sure, there's a sheriff. There's even a jail. The sheriff knows what's good for him so he does what he's told."

Hemingway walked away. The boy looked after his father. He didn't smile when he nodded to Latigo. "Thanks for listening, mister," he said. "All I wanted was for somebody else to know about it."

"That helps," said Latigo and called his horse. He swung a leg across the saddle. "Where you headed now, Buck?"

The youth hung thumbs in his belt, light strong on his long face and yellow hair, and shrugged. "Farther west, I guess. Maybe north. Don't seem to matter much. This is where we'd like to be. You heard what Pa said. We've been here twenty years. Guess I was here before I was born."

Latigo tugged up the gelding's head. "Don't see how I can help, Buck. Would if I could."

Buck agreed. "I guess nobody can. Kincaid's a big man."

"Thanks for the water."

The young fellow watched Latigo turn the horse. "You're welcome. What's your name, mister?"

Latigo looked down. "Lansen," I said.

At the buckboard Hemingway raised his face to the light. "Why'd you come riding this way, son?"

The sun was also in Latigo's eyes. He tilted his hat forward and threaded rein leather through his fingers. "Own some land around here," he said. "From what I remember, this was a good place to live."

"Keep riding, boy. They'll have you out inside weeks."

"Maybe not," Latigo said and thought about it. "Thanks for the water. My compliments to Mrs. Hemingway."

" 'Bye, son."

Buck watched until Latigo was out of sight. His father addressed him and had to speak his name twice.

Latigo rode across flats and came to the stream. Aspen and toyon berry grew close to the water. He reined at the two marked graves and looked back. Twenty years, he thought. He drew the Winchester from the scabbard and laid the gun across his thighs. Twenty years is a lifetime. Buck had been here before he was born.

Four miles nearer the Gila river wind raised sand and dust in a cloud. He walked the gelding through patches of big-eared cactus that stood out like dead men or prairie witches with reaching hands, and waited for the wagon to come abreast out of the haze.

The people on board weren't old, the driver deep-chested, the woman round-faced and buxom. The man hauled on the reins and the team slowed to a halt. Flying sand beat against Latigo's ears. He touched his hat to the woman. The man eyed him before nodding. The wagon was piled high with furniture and bedding. Latigo edged the gelding closer as the driver tipped his hat to keep off the wind. "Howdy, stranger."

"Howdy!" returned Latigo, voice loud. "Don't figure to find out what's none of my business, mister, but are you folks moving out of Gila valley?"

"That's what we're doing, stranger."

Latigo bent his head and shouted. "You being driven out?" he asked. "Like the Hemingways?"

The driver unbuttoned his coat to uncover the gun he wore. "Don't reckon a man has to tell his business to every stranger he meets," he said.

"I'm not a stranger, mister," corrected Latigo. "You don't need to show your gun. I got an interest hereabouts and I aim to find out only what's good for me."

"We're leaving because there's no future here for a man who can't hire himself ten pairs of guns."

The woman touched the man's arm. "We don't aim to do any fighting, mister," she said, concern but no cowardice in her voice. "Jed and me ... we're not married very long. We haven't had our firstborn yet."

"Are you being driven out?" repeated Latigo. "I'm not belittling you, mister. All I asked was were you being driven out of Gila river valley?"

The man worked with the reins in his hands. He spat over the side and eyed Latigo. "Sold my land legal," he said crossly.

Dust made the saguarro loom like yellow wraiths. The gelding was impatient. Latigo tightened rein and slapped a leg on flank. Then the wind died, the whine and whistle eased and red and pink cactus blossom bloomed big and rich again. "All I want to know is how to protect myself," he explained.

The man on the wagon leaned forward. The hostility

10

left his face. He regarded Latigo with interest. "You know this country, mister?" he asked.

"Know Gila river country," said Latigo.

The woman spoke. "Then you know what's happening."

Latigo shook his head. "No, ma'am, I don't. This here's my home ground and I'm coming back. Rode past the Hemingways' place a little while ago and they were pulling out. Then I meet you and you're doing the same thing. I'm tired riding a horse, want to stand on the ground. I'd like to know what I'm up against."

The driver of the wagon eyed him levelly. "Kincaid's his name. He's driving everybody out."

"Everybody?"

"He's got hired guns, mister. The way it is now the fellow who points a gun at you is right. Never met the man yet who could talk back to the end of a shooting iron. With us it was easy. I was a small man, didn't have much stake."

"Thanks," said Latigo. "I'm obliged to you."

"Glad to meet with you," said the woman.

The man beat dust out of his clothes with the flat of his hat. "You're not wearing guns," he said. "That's the first thing I'd think about if I was you."

"I'll take care of it."

Sand fell from wheel rims as the wagon moved. The man leaned over to speak again. "See any Indians on your way?"

"Killed one yesterday."

"You figure they're running wild?"

"There's a big peace being made. If it works out the Apache will be over in Chiricahua country, near the mountains."

"Reckon we'll be all right, then."

"Keep your gun handy."

"Sure will. Glad to have words with you, stranger."

Latigo backed away and turned the gelding. The wagon moved on. None of it was good.

The air was bright after the wind and sand, cactus scents reaching out like a lure. He rode sideways across a slope of land. Bluestem grass appeared underfoot and he began to think he could smell the river. He sat up straight, searching ahead. He knew this ground, had hoofed it a hundred times, riding bareback on a long-geared colt with-

11

out a bridle, using hands on a mane-hold and tight legs to stay mounted. When he saw the river he dug in his heels and raced and whatever it was that stretched his spine, squared his shoulders and tightened chest and knuckles, the gelding felt it, too.

The Gila river, which is like the veins on the back of a man's hand, begins near the Black mountains of New Mexico somewhere west of Socorro, sucks at the earth of Arizona in a network of tributaries like the roots of a tree and heads west in a twisting swirl for only less than a thousand miles. The Santa Cruz helps feed the rushing water from the south as do the Salt and Verde rivers which swell into the Gila from the north and join the southewestern flow not far from Phoenix.

For Latigo, who at El Paso had looked across the Rio Grande and in the north had seen the Colorado, the Gila was the only river in the world; blue as the sky in high clear daylight, shining like silver at night, making a wind of air and a rushing sound that was like the ringing of bells.

He flung aside his hat and walked into the water, boots and all, to wet hands and face and head. It tasted the same, was the same water, the same river. Gila Bend wasn't far away now. He stared at the sky till body heat and sun dried skin and shirt. When he rode again he hurried, skirted the river for a time, finally moved to higher ground.

He was still thinking of the river when the dark-haired girl on a pony climbed the sloping ground and rode quickly out of sight. Two men met on horseback, dismounted, left the horses where they stood and, without speaking, began to fight. Latigo quickened and rode close. He reached for the rifle and thought better of it. He looked over his shoulder for the girl but she did not reappear.

The men weren't evenly matched. One was older and solid and knew how to handle his weight so that the other fellow knew what hit him. He was a square-faced man with a full broad moustache and wide shoulders. His lips were tight, his face angry.

The younger man was Latigo's height and weight, skin dark and clear, face well shaped and handsome. His hair was black as tar and his good looks and flat waist might have come from Mexican blood. He held himself well and had a tight lean frame. Nobody spoke. Latigo watched.

12

The fight was hard and clean and serious, without boots or knee work. The two men rolled on the ground, stood up, used their fists and knocked each other down, grunted and spat blood. The young fellow's face bled first but he straightened again every time he fell down. The bigger man had punch and longer arms. When the struggle moved close to where Latigo sat on the horse and the gelding backed away, head in the air, neither of the men slowed. Knowing that he was there didn't stop the fight which was private and important.

The big man hit the young fellow and he went down to lie on his back, gasping, legs all spread out, chest flat, shoulders trying to rise and not having the strength. His eye was cut and his cheek bloodmarked. In a minute he turned on his belly, pressed himself up and rose. The other man waited and the lean-bodied younger man came running to swipe at the man with the moustache. It was a good hit and the big fellow reeled back but did not fall down. He rushed in again with a clenched, clasped-fist pole-axe that missed. The young dark man stepped out of the path of the swish of air and bone.

Then something else happened. Hoofbeats drummed on the air and another rider raced down from high ground. The fighting men heard the sounds of the horse and the young fellow's shoulders squared. He hardened and hit the big man twice, blows that made the man with the moustache stand back and suck in wind. But it was only for a minute. The big fellow hit the younger man a crunching, bone-breaking blow that ended the fight, a pile-driver that filled the dark-skinned man's sky with stars and turned the daylight black. The young fellow choked and fell down and this time he didn't get up. He had been hurt. He twisted on the ground, body bent like a jack-knife, and groaned. The big fellow wiped his mouth and stood back.

The rider came close. Latigo reached for the gun a second time and then saw her yellow hair. She approached like a storm of wind on a fine-limbered mare, all haste and purpose, slowed and slid from the saddle as easily and smoothly as any young buck who might throw his leg forward across his pony's mane and dismount from a saddle-less horse in one beautiful, boneless motion. She carried a riding whip and her eyes were on fire. Fine golden hair showed under her flat-topped Mexican sombrero. She saw nobody but the man on the ground. Latigo watched as she ran to the young fellow.

At times like this a man doesn't much care who his company is. He shows what he feels. The spare-bodied man was hurt and not ashamed of it. There was blood on his face, his chest hurt and his hands shook. The woman knelt on the ground by his side, raised his head from the dirt and brushed his forehead with her fingers. He was too hurt to know. Her eyes moved quickly over his face. She spoke his name and he only groaned. She tried to raise him up and failed. Then she rose, eyes bright, lips tight and hands clenched.

The man with the moustache picked up his hat. When he straightened the riding crop cut him across the face. He started back, angry and surprised. She did it again, eyes dancing in fury, voice as sharp as the whiplash. He snatched the crop from her hand and his broad face darkened as red weals appeared. He raised the whip to strike her in return and Latigo's hand moved to the rifle stock. He didn't have to slide the gun from the holster for the wide-faced man only glared at the woman and tossed the whip aside. "Ask him!" he said loudly. "He saw it all. It was a fair fight and Joe got what was coming to him! Go on, ask the man on the horse!"

Latigo's forehead creased. He stepped down. The man with the whip-marked face strode to his horse, mounted, walked the animal back and spoke down to her, finger pointing. "Some day," he said hoarsely. "I'll kill him . . . and I won't be gentle! Tell him that!" He spurred the mount and rode away. Latigo's eyes came back to the woman. He waited to be asked.

She turned and stared hard at him. She had a fine lovely face, red lips that were tight now with suppressed fury, and eyes that were too dark for such light coloured hair. Her breasts moved under a yellow buckskin jacket and her riding skirt flared away from a narrow waist. She wore fancy riding boots of polished brown leather and was the finest looking woman he'd seen. When she did not speak he confirmed what the older man had said. "What the man says is true, ma'am. It was a fair fight."

Her eyes glittered. "You saw it all?" she asked.

"Yes, ma'am."

"Why didn't you do something?"

"Like what, ma'am?"

"You could have stopped them!"

Her hands and body quivered. She wanted to whip him also but the crop lay on the ground. "They didn't want to be stopped," Latigo said quietly. "Looked to me they had good reason for fighting."

"You were afraid!" she accused. His legs straightened and his shoulders rose. "You see a man beaten nearly to death and you don't lift a finger to help! What kind of man are you?"

He eyed her calmly, was slow to speak. Her flushed cheeks made her beautiful, a fiery beauty, all flame and temper. "Ma'am," he said, "I've done all the fighting for other people I'm going to do. A man's got a right to mind his own business."

Her lips compressed. "You're a coward!" she said and watched his jaw harden. "Who are you, anyway? What are you doing here?"

He moved to the horse, gathered up the rein and regarded her. "Nothing in the world so hard to put up with, ma'am, as a stiff-necked woman," he said. "I reckon you talk the way you do because nobody ever told you not to."

She had stepped nearer the man on the ground, moving his arms now and trying to rise. As Latigo spoke she turned quickly, eyes still alight with the old anger and sharpened with a new. "What did you say?" she demanded.

"You're talking out of turn, ma'am."

Her hands clenched again. The quirt lay too far away. Her breasts rose. "How dare you!" she cried.

He nodded. "That's what I mean, ma'am."

He raised himself into the saddle and threaded reins. The gelding came round. "Aren't you going to help him up?" she asked, the words stinging. "You can see he's hurt!"

"No, ma'am. He fell down by himself. Let him get up by himself."

She turned from him, trembling, furious in defeat. She watched as he walked the horse away. The sun was strong, the light from the west, and he wore the hat forward to shield his eyes. There was an ease in the way he sat on the horse, in the way he ignored her and in the shape of his shoulders that was masculine and had nothing to do with her kind of pride. She did not know what to think. She did not understand her own confusion and didn't know why not.

The young fellow on the ground moved and made a sound. She knelt and helped him to rise. Blood from the cut over his eye had hardened on his cheekbone, his chin was bruised and his lips swollen. He swayed and held her arm. She thought about the man on the horse. She looked again. Latigo was moving away. "What were you fighting about, Joe?" she asked.

The dark-skinned man brushed his mouth and squinted in the sunlight, eyes following the straight-backed figure on the gelding. "Nothing," he said. "It was just a fight."

She made him look at her. "Joe, it wasn't just a fight," she said. "I want to know!"

"It was just a fight, Hildy," he said crossly. "A man-fight that doesn't have anything to do with you. A fellow needs a fight sometimes. You don't know . . ." She slapped his cheek and his dark face smarted. "If you'd marry me, I wouldn't have to fight," he said.

She knew that and didn't answer him. He reached for her hands and she avoided the touch. His eyes sulked. "Get on your horse, Joe," she said. "Father wants you."

"What for?"

Again her eyes sought the shape of the man on the gelding, still visible, distant now. "I don't know. He just wants you."

He walked to his horse. She picked up the crop. When she was mounted she asked, "Who was that stranger, Joe?"

He followed Latigo's direction; a man on a horse, dark against yellow grass, too far away to be recognised. "Never saw him before. Some cowhand. I reckon."

"What's he doing here? Is he looking for work?"

"I told you. I never saw the fellow before."

"He could have stopped the fight."

"No!" he said sharply." "I didn't want the fight stopped. I'm not finished with Nevin. I'll kill him!"

"That's what he said about you, "Joe," she remembered. Her eyes met his. Her look was distant and deep. "Why were you fighting?"

He didn't answer. He spurred the horse forward. "Come on, we'd better get back. I'm in enough trouble already."

16

Together they rode over sunlit grass. She remembered the face of Latigo Lansen and his lips, his hands when he straightened the rein and gripped the saddle horn, and eyes that weren't afraid of her. The man riding by her side was as tall, as straight, and knew how to sit on a horse but there was a difference that had nothing to do with the shape of either or how each man rode a horse. She didn't know what it was and not knowing disturbed her.

CHAPTER TWO

GILA Bend hadn't changed much. What was new Latigo noticed at once. The bank was brick and plaster now and the church had been painted white. The boardwalk followed the corner of the bank and turned east. The day was still bright, shades were drawn, window glass glinted in the light, the street between unpainted frame buildings caked mud, rutted by a thousand wheel rims. He walked the gelding, looking for faces that he knew. Nobody waved a hat or cried his name. Coming back wasn't what he had expected.

At the blacksmith's, where he watered the horse, a round-faced sweating man in a split leather apron strode out into the light. "Something I can do for you, mister?"

"Was looking for the Land Office," said Latigo. "Figured it was over by the bank."

"Used to be, then the bank got bigger. Land Office moved. Keep going the way you're headed. It's up by the sheriff's office."

"Thanks."

The blacksmith wiped his red face. "If you're looking for work, son," he said. "Kincaid is the man to see."

"Hear he's the big man in these parts."

The man on the ground nodded. "Sure," he said. "He's big but he's not any bigger than the boots he wears. Doesn't affect me none. If a man rides a horse he's got to come to me. Could give you a job myself, if you know anything about smithy work."

"Right now I'm not looking for work," said Latigo. "Besides, what I know most about's not in your line."

17

"What do you know about, mister?"

"Cattle," said Latigo. "Horses . . . know some about guns, too."

The smith looked him over quickly. "You another hired gun?" he asked sharply.

"No."

"How come you're not wearing guns?"

"I'm a peaceable man. Didn't know I'd need to." Latigo touched his hat. "Thanks for the information. When my horse needs looking at I'll bring him in."

"Sure. Have to wait your turn."

Four men walked out of the sheriff's office into the light. All of them wore guns. The sheriff followed and stood on the boardwalk. Three of the men were young lean-bodied fellows with straight backs and narrow jaws. Latigo idled his horse and watched the dark man with the sullen good looks who had come out second best in the fight. Since then he'd washed his face and there was no blood on his lips but the marks of another man's fist remained. All three men seemed of an age. Hired guns, he thought.

The fourth was older, used to the sun, smooth-faced and clean-shaven. His voice was strong with authority. His boots were polished and the white shirt he wore clean that morning. "You tell the judge what I said," he ordered and hoisted himself into the saddle.

The sheriff was quick to speak. "Yes, Mister Kincaid, I'll tell him. I'll go see him right away."

"It's got to be done legal, you understand."

This was Kincaid. Latigo Lansen watched, searching for the known signs of land hunger; eyes with the strangeness of distance in them, pupils that held on to what they saw with greed and grasp and shone with a pointed light, the restlessness that came out in hands and shoulders and the curious need for haste.

There were no such marks upon the man. He had a powerful body and strong chin. He looked like an important cattleman and not like anything else.

All four mounted and wheeled from the rail. The dark man stared at Latigo on the gelding. Neither spoke. Latigo turned away. The fellow spurred his horse and followed the others. Once he looked back over his shoulders, face clouded in doubt. Latigo made no sign. He watched their dust.

The sheriff stepped out of the shade. He eyed Latigo and the gelding. "You looking for something, stranger?"

"Land Office," said Latigo.

The sheriff was about to point and then didn't. "I'm sheriff around here," he announced. "What kind of business you aim to do at the Land Office?"

"Some looking."

"Looking for what? I got a right to know, mister."

"Wanted to find out if the Lansen ranch is still where it ought to be."

The sheriff looked up. "Lansen . . . ? Yeh, it's still there. South of town by the river. Won't do you any good, though. Lansen's been dead a long time."

"He has a son."

"Killed in the war. If you're looking for work, ride out to the Kincaid place. Tell them the sheriff sent you."

"Thanks, Sheriff. I'm not looking for work. I'm looking for the Land Office."

The sheriff's face tightened. Latigo did not look away nor did the lawman. "Pays to be civil around here, stranger. I'm the sheriff."

"I know. You're wearing the badge."

"We don't much like strangers who talk out of turn."

"I didn't start the talk, Sheriff. You did."

"Just where'd you come from, mister?"

"Apache country."

"See any redskins?"

"Killed one."

"You're not wearing guns. Kill him with the rifle?"

"No. Killed him with my hands."

"You mean to say you got close enough to an Apache to kill him with your hands?"

"My hand had a knife in it, Sheriff."

The sheriff hitched his gunbelt. "You talk real fancy, mister," he said. "But you don't look like any card player."

"Never played cards in my whole life."

"What're you doing here, then? You're not looking for work and you don't play cards!"

"Looking for the Land Office, Sheriff."

The lawman turned away. "Right behind you," he threw back. Latigo watched him disappear and the door close.

Kincaid had looked honest, too. He stepped down from the horse.

The clerk in the Land Office wore spectacles.

"What can I do for you, mister?"

"Want to confirm a title."

The clerk produced a thick wide volume and laid the book on the counter. "Folio number and date," he demanded. Latigo spread his parchment on the counter. "Eighteen-fifty three," mused the clerk. "Gadsden Purchase land." He looked up. "You Latimer Lansen?"

"That's right."

The clerk was satisfied. "It's your land," he said. "No impediment at all. Certificate includes water rights in perpetuity—that means forever—or as long as the Gila river runs. Good for collateral, mortgage or bank loans. Any time you feel like selling, you're free to do that."

Latigo pocketed the papers. "I won't be selling," he said.

The thin-faced man studied him over the rims of the spectacles. "Why'd you confirm your title?"

"To make sure it's mine."

"What're you figuring on doing?"

"Land should be worked. I aim to do that."

"Cattle?"

"This is cattle country."

The clerk closed the register. He regarded Latigo soberly. "You want some advice, son?"

Latigo returned the regard. "Only a fool doesn't want advice."

The man's lips puckered. "Most times around here it pays to wear a gun. Two, if you can use both hands."

The blacksmith had noted that he didn't wear sidearms, then the sheriff and now the land clerk. There had been the deep-chested man on the wagon, too.

"Especially now," said the man with glasses. "I've had this book open plenty of times lately. Seems to me if I owned any land around here I'd take good care of myself. I'd sure enough learn how to shoot."

"How much time you think I've got to learn?"

"No telling," said the clerk. "No telling at all, now that you're here."

"You mean I should have stayed away?"

"Should have learned how to shoot before you came."

20

"Is there a gunsmith in Gila Bend?"

"No. But there's a general store down the street a piece from the bank. Ed Harrison sells most everything. Besides, a man looks better wearing a gun. If he's got the shape for it, I mean. Looks better when he's riding a horse, too."

"Good advice," said Latigo. "I'm obliged to you."

The clerk's face brightened. "You figuring on wearing guns?"

"Wouldn't want to be thought a fool, mister."

"Mallow's the name . . . John Mallow."

At the door Latigo looked back. "Why'd you tell me?"

The land clerk shrugged. "Hate to see a young fellow get hurt, that's all," he said. "Honest advice doesn't cost anything. I'm just a land clerk. Maybe that's all I can give."

"It's more than you think."

The sheriff's office was stone and brick built with iron bars across the windows. The door lay open because of the heat. Inside the building was shaded. Latigo entered and the sheriff straightened. "Day, Sheriff . . ."

The lawman nodded shortly. "What can I do for you?"

"Like to talk some."

"Busy right now. Got a lot of work to do. If I was you, mister, I'd keep on riding. This town's open at both ends."

"Rode a long way to get here, Sheriff. Gila Bend is the end of my journey."

The other man's eyebrows went up. "What're you talking about?"

"I figured on staying, Sheriff," Latigo announced. "Soon as I get a gun to wear."

Impatience edged the sheriff's voice. He was a big man, had once been strong. "Look, mister," he said. "We don't like smart-talking strangers around here. If you've got something to say, you say it then start riding."

"Not a stranger, Sheriff," said Latigo. "And I don't figure on doing much more riding. I was born here, belong here."

The lawman stared hard at him, from forehead to boots and back again. Recognition did not light his face. "Never saw you before," he said. "Been here nine years, know everybody in these parts."

"The name's Lansen, Sheriff."

21

The sheriff's shoulders stiffened. Latigo held out the land deed so that it could be read without being touched. The lawman's eyes moved down the paper and halted at the name of the owner. He looked up slowly. "You were supposed to be dead," he said.

Latigo put the paper away. "Lots of men died at Vicksburg," he said. "Land office is satisfied I'm not one of them."

The man with the badge on his shirtfront sat back in his chair. "All right," he said. "The paper says you're Latimer Lansen. What do you want from me?"

"Protection."

"From what?"

"Don't know, Sheriff. Plan to work my land and raise cattle. Want the law on my side, that's all."

"The sheriff's on the side of every law-abiding citizen in the county, mister."

"That's what I wanted to hear, Sheriff," said Latigo and walked to the door, glad of sunlight.

The sheriff was alone. He stared at the green-shaded oil lamp on the desk, pushed a gun into holster and rose. He walked straight to the Land Office. "Young fellow in here a while ago, name of Lansen . . ."

"That's right, Sheriff. Confirming ownership of the Lansen ranch."

"Was it in order?"

"Surest thing you know, Sheriff. Nobody owns that land but that young man. Sort of figure he's going to keep on owning it, too."

"Was it notarised?"

"All down in black and white. Signed by a judge. The land is his, Sheriff. River land . . ."

John Mallow watched the sheriff out of the office, stayed watching the door even when the man with the badge had gone. When he had pushed the book back into its place on the shelf he stood at the small window and watched Latigo Lansen walk his horse slowly along by the river, moving south. Shadows and hazing outlines warned that night had begun to claim the sky. He reckoned that the flat-waisted man on the horse would bed down somewhere for the night and ride to the ranch first thing in the morning. He'd want to see it in the early light. After ten years, morning was the best time.

22

Latigo laid a trail over the range and reined when he came in sight of the house. His throat tightened. The gelding stretched the rein to nibble at grass, sniffed air and smelled water. He was alone on the sloping land with the sun in the east and shadow reaching away from him. This was the time for crying out and he remained silent.

Smoke hadn't risen from the chimney in eight years and that was a long time for a house to be without a fire. A house is not a home until logs are burning on the hearth and feet walking on board floors, until windows shine and the door stays open.

A windbreak of alder and larch rose behind the house and hid the bunkhouse. Five men used to sleep there. Out in front of the house stood the water butt and pump. Two hundred yards farther on the river ran sheathed with sunlight. From the house you could see clear down to the water, not a bush or a tree in the way.

Apache Indians had ridden across this land after buffalo or in the pursuit of war, with painted skins, wearing feathers and wielding lances and the air still echoed to the sound of their cries, the beat of drums and the music of thin reed pipes that made big medicine and was magic. Blood had been spilt and the last Apache lance to pierce the earth only ten yards from the front of the house still stood in a circle of whitened stones, the feathers shrivelled but the lance itself a lonely and barbaric reminder of wind and war on grassy plains and of history in the making.

Latigo looked away. It is only when there are people present to make a welcome of human sound that a man feels like crying out. When he is alone the urge is gone and and he should have known this.

The windows were dusty and the pine log door creaked when he let in the light. His shadow rushed ahead of him into the house. There were no ghosts to rear up at him and he was glad. Jeremiah Lansen had not even died in the house and the memories contained within the four walls were living thoughts.

The gelding came to the open door and kept an eye on him, watching his movements, listening for the sounds he made, being curious and puzzled when he was silent.

The doors and windows he opened wide. The bedding he burned in a smoky bonfire that sent a yellow-black coil into the sky. He inspected the corral and set fallen rails back in place. He rode north and found the stone marker with the name 'LANSEN' cut in granite. He turned east and rode until he found another, then south to where the hand of Lansen still clung to the earth. There were no fences anywhere to enclose the wide ranges of hard buffalo grass. Aspen clothed the river edges and willow slanted out over the water. It was all that he expected and it was intact. He could live with everything he saw and he was at a good age to start living.

The first thing to buy was a gun to buckle to his hip.

When the hooves of a single rider beat on the ground Latigo walked out into sunlight. The rider swept up the draw and reined within yards of the house. He was young, hard-faced and lean, like any one of the three who had ridden away from the sheriff's office. He sat upright in the saddle while Latigo approached then leaned forward, elbow on the horn, and stared, eyes deepset under straight eyebrows but cold, his brown-skinned face clear and lighted. Latigo was sure he was one of the three, all had the same empty depth about the eyes, all seemed ready to squeeze the trigger, all had the look that came from never trusting, never being trusted.

"What can I do for you, stranger?"

He had placed the Winchester rifle in the gun rack inside the door, his first act of possession, so he was unarmed. The man on the horse wore a gun on each thigh. The rider stared, not taking his eyes from Latigo's face. He straightened and clasped the saddle horn with both hands. "You the owner around here?" he asked; a question only, with no real interest in any kind of answer.

"That's right."

"Name of Lansen?"

"Something you want?"

"I got what I came for, Mister Lansen."

Latigo stood forward and looked up so the man on the horse could see his face. "A good look at me. Is that what you came for?"

The rider did not answer. He stared longer then wheeled the horse. Latigo watched him ride down the draw and out of sight. He whistled and the gelding stretched a long neck out over the corral fence. He carried the saddle to the rail.

At the livery stable he said: "Can I borrow your buck-board? Got lots of stuff to hitch out."

"Where you at, mister?"

"Lansen ranch."

"Sure. Hitch up one of the work horses. You'll find the wagon out back."

In the general store Ed Harrison listened and nodded his head. "Can give you almost any kind of gun being used. You name it, mister. Almost sure to have it."

"A Colt would suit."

"Got a real nice pistol handy. Reckon one's all you want."

"Only takes one gun to kill a man."

"Who're you aiming to kill, son?"

"The fellow who's aiming to kill me."

"You're sure somebody is?"

"It'll turn out that way."

Harrison laid the Colt six-gun on the glass-topped showcase and moved to the front of the store as the door-bell tinkled. Latigo selected a gunbelt and buckled the leather so the hang and feel were right. He was opening the chamber of the gun when the fair-haired woman came in and he turned to wait and to watch. There was no fury behind her eyes. She did not wear a hat and her yellow hair was plaited in a thick rope and bound up at the back. She wore a short fringed and beaded buckskin jacket and was still the finest looking woman he'd seen.

But she rode a high horse. Someday somebody would take her down a peg or two and when it happened dust would cloud the air inside the corral and there'd be noise and anger and she'd be hurt. He looked away before their eyes could meet.

"Father needs tobacco," she said carelessly to Harrison.

Latigo picked up bullets and handled the six-gun. She walked to where he stood. "There's something I'd like to know," she said.

He touched his hat to her. "Yes, ma'am?"

"You saw the fight yesterday, Joe Erskine and Ben Nevin . . ."

"Yes, ma'am. I saw the fight."

She remembered what he had said to her, how he had looked at her and the movement of his body as he swung himself easily up into the saddle. She had been troubled all day afterwards because she wasn't sure that he was only what he looked like, a cowhand on a horse, something you see every day of the year; men who rode from town to town or spread to spread for sometimes less than thirty dollars a month and keep, putting down no roots, running with the cattle, growing lean and hard and lined and, with loneliness shining out of their eyes, being spoiled forever for anything else because the promise of men had been beaten out of them. So far he hadn't been to the ranch to ask for work but if he was a cowhand he would come. They always did.

"What were they fighting about?"

"Didn't ask, ma'am."

"But you were there. You saw it."

"Still didn't ask. Figured it was none of my business."

"It's my business," she said sharply.

He ignored the heat in her voice and the ring of command. He thrust a bullet into the chamber with unusual slowness. "That doesn't make it mine, ma'am."

She could have been angered by that and chose not to be though the edge on her voice remained.

"Did you see anything . . . and don't tell me you saw them fighting. I know that much."

The feel of the pistol was smooth and clean and comforting, different from the Winchester; closer to you and more like a part of you; an arm, maybe, or a hand. In Gila Bend a gun could be a friend.

"Saw what I was looking at."

Her breasts rose with a sharp intake of breath. He found her eyes uncertain, ready to be exasperated but afraid. "You're not on a horse now, ma'am," he said calmly. "Wouldn't talk down to people if I were you."

She didn't look away and the wrath didn't rise. "Are you a cowhand, looking for work? If you are I can help you."

"No, ma'am."

She was disappointed. "You're stubborn!" she said.

He nodded. "Yes, ma'am. I'm stubborn."

"I've broken horses before, mister!"

He placed the last bullet and with a twist of the fingers spun the chamber. "Ever break men?"

Her eyes did not leave his face. She should have flared up by now. He was surprised that she hadn't. "Yes," she

26

said slowly. "I've broken men. I did it with a whip in my hand."

"I guess they never fought back, ma'am."

"I had the whip!"

He recognised the barrier of starch and stubbornness between them, a barrier he could walk away from but which imprisoned her because there was something on his side that she wanted. That put him on the horse and the woman on the ground. Her face didn't change at all when she spoke again but her voice was different.

"Was there . . ." she asked. "Was there . . . a woman present?"

That changed things. She was a woman after all, not so high, not so mighty as she appeared, like all women who were uncertain or with cause for jealousy, sheltering behind the armour of pride. But now, because this was something she needed to know, she will willing to step from behind the shield and ask.

Joe was the good-looking man and he had an eye for the dark girl on the horse. The man with the moustache could be the girl's father and that might mean that Joe wasn't welcome in one quarter and forbidden from another.

This woman wasn't sure of herself, or of Joe.

"I'm a stranger here, ma'am," Latigo said deliberately. "Don't know anything about a woman."

The anger came back with a rush, stronger for being held down. Her eyes blazed and his cheek stung when she slapped his face.

"You're a liar!" she said.

He watched her out of the store and past the window, his face smarting. Ed Harrison came round to the gun counter. "Heard the last part of it," he said. "I liked the bits with the venom in them."

"I'll take the Colt," said Latigo.

"Suits you. Sam Colt's a busy man these days. Want something else?"

"Got a list of things here. Make it up while I fetch the buckboard."

"Sure. You figuring on staying a while?"

"I'll be here for a long time."

"You want I should open an account with you? This here's quite a list."

"You trust me?"

"Never saw you before but you sure wouldn't want all this stuff unless you were planning to stay. If you aim to stay then I reckon you also aim to pay your bills. I'll put your name down in the book. What're you called, mister?"

"Lansen."

Ed Harrison's eyes were sharp. "You Jeremiah Lansen's boy?" he asked. Latigo nodded. The big storekeeper looked at him. "That why you bought the gun?"

"No," answered Latigo. "Vanity, pure and simple. John Mallow down at the land office said I'd look better wearing a gun."

Harrison eyed the gunbelt. "He was right, mister. You do look better. You know who that high-stepping filly is who just slapped your face?"

"Somebody important?"

"Hildy Kincaid. Her father owns most of the valley by now. Pity she's so uppity. Best looking woman hereabouts."

Hildy Kincaid and Joe, thought Latigo. Her father owns the valley and Joe looks like a cowhand. It didn't seem right. "Where does Joe come into it?" he asked.

"He's Kincaid's foreman."

"They're more than friends, I'd say."

"You might be wrong," differed Harrison. "Joe wants to be more than friends. Fact is, he wants to marry Hildy."

"And she doesn't?"

"Seems to me like she's not sure. Reckon she wants to get married all right but maybe she doesn't want it to be Joe."

"She keeps a pretty tight rein on him."

"That's because he does what she tells him. He knows what's good for him. The way I figure it, Joe's not the man she really wants."

"Why not? He's beautiful."

Harrison ruminated, pursed his lips. "Strange thing about Joe, mister. Good cowpoke, good foreman, good with guns, always looking for a fight, but he never broke a horse in his life. And she sure is uppity."

It came out without thought. He didn't know he was going to say it. "You reckon there'd be a chance for somebody else?" asked Latigo.

Harrison nodded. "For the fellow who can tame a

28

horse, son, I'd say there was lots more than just a chance."
Latigo walked to the door and the storekeeper spoke again.
"You do look better wearing a gun, mister."

"Latigo's the name. Latigo Lansen."

He loaded the buckboard and started for home knowing
that he would itch all night in new blankets and maybe not
sleep on the mattress. The gelding trotted alongside the
wagon.

The sky was westering when he reached the ranch, calm
and still in a breathlessness that reached back through the
furrow of years to when the first light paled the dark and
rushed forward into years not yet spent for its effects of
magnitude and wonder. Soon his thin column of blue
smoke rose from the stone chimney into the vastness
above. Even the river was silent in the face of heaven-
burning glory. Creation displayed itself in every variation
of splendour, for him alone it seemed, since he had the
world to himself.

The narrow shadow of the Apache lance traversed the
circle of whitened stones, faded and disappeared. Darkness came, then bright moonlight. When the shadow of the
lance appeared again in ghostly white radiance from the
night sky Latigo raised his head from the pillow and
listened.

The house was still and silent. There was no creaking
of wood. There was hardly a rustle of wind in the alder
and larch behind the house. Then he heard it again.

The sound of horses.

CHAPTER THREE

SHARP edges of sound ripped the silence. Pistol shots
burst in pointed explosions of light and bullets whanged
against stone walls. Latigo leaped from the bed and tugged
on pants, naked otherwise. He heard shouts and the noise
of running hooves. His own gelding whinnied shrilly from
the corral.

He ran to the rack by the door and snatched down the
Winchester. The noise outside became a rushing haze of
shouts and shots and stamping hoofbeats. He crawled to

the window and raised his head. Bullets spattered in leaden rain above him and glass splintered inwards. He sat on his haunches, shoulders on cold stone and listened. In the darkness the noise continued. He bent his body low and ran to the bedroom for the pistol, gun metal suddenly chill between belly and belt. Outside the torrent of sound coiled up in a whirlpool about the ranch-house. He moved to the window and jacked the rifle.

Wraithlike shapes of men on horses reared up in moon-lighted darkness, prancing and stamping, arms waving, guns exploding, wearing the night like a shroud. Ground was pawed and hoofed till dust rose in a mist.

Glass burst away from wooden window frames. Daggers of light stabbed the dark. Latigo ran from window to window, gun ready, seeking a target, standing back flat against the front wall of the house and snatching only a glance out into the night, crouching low when breaking glass sliced the air, finding the gunstock warm in moistened palms and feeling a ridge of cold across his shoulders.

There might be ten of them out there and he saw none of their faces. They made dust and used it as a shield. Bullets sloughed into roof shingles, whanged and flattened on sudden stone barriers: Jagged slivers of resined wood leaped from the inside of the pine log door and the mirror in the room where he slept broke apart into a thousand glittering edges.

He splintered glass, pushed the rifle barrel through the frame and squeezed the trigger, jacked and squeezed. Hoarse, angry shouts greeted his response and a hail of bullets rained upon the window. He stood to the side and waited, face sweating. Glass danced away from grooved wood and scattered on the floor. Bullets whipped through the darkness of the room. Dishes fell with a clatter from the rack.

He rolled on the floor from one window to the other and used the Colt. Six bullets sped out into dusty moon-light and clouded darkness. The gelding whinnied and he damned it to silence. He used the Winchester in a rapid succession of shots that killed nobody. He haunched to the bedroom. Lying on his back he loaded both guns.

Outside, the raiders careered in a circle about the house, dust from hooves rising in a swirling cloud. Latigo slammed at the glass of the bedroom window with the rifle barrel and straightened, gun against bare shoulder, only a glimmer of moonlight on his chest.

Horsemen swept past the window; noisy, formless shapes of dark, rushing out of blackness, stamping on in swift succession or coming lumped together in reaching twos and threes. He emptied the rifle, ran to the front of the house and used the Colt as men on horses cleaved dusty darkness. His skin shone with sweat, he had hit nobody and hadn't bought enough shells.

He scuppered to the bedroom, lay on his back by the side of the bed to fill the guns and felt the sting of slivered glass on shoulder-blades. From the window he watched mounted men swerve and gallop. Horses arched and rose in the air to leap the fence in a savage black poetry accompanied by yelling voices, the beat of hooves on dry earth and the spit of guns. Unlighted bodies, and legs and tail and flying manes, sprang from shadow into flight, stamped and churned the ground and reached wildly on.

He waited for a rider to be silhouetted, dark against deeper dark, fired and wasted the lead. The horse raced on and bullets whistled back at him.

He heard the grind and twist of wood as the water butt and upright pump were dragged at the end of ropes. He jacked the rifle and aimed at hazy figures on phantom horses. Lariats snaked out about fence posts. Corral rails fell with a clatter. The gelding nickered, stamped and fought murky air, eyes wild, ears high. The workhorse ran in circles as the gelding wheeled, trumpeted, leaped the broken rails and hoofed into the night.

Then suddenly it was all over, the horsemen racing to the river, the darkness empty of pistol shots. Latigo flung open the door and ran out, barefooted, rifle to shoulder, shooting at targets enveloped in a screen of flying dust. The raiders reached the river and splurged into water. Latigo used the Colt and when the weapon was empty flung it aside. Naked to the waist he stood at the edge of the seething river and pointed the rifle.

Churned up water followed the horsemen to the other side. A round bright moon hung in the sky. Latigo took his time and was careful. He squeezed the trigger and watched a dark figure sag and sway in the saddle. A cry rose above the sounds of horses, men, bubbling water and bullets. Lead sang in the air. Latigo flung himself down

31

and hugged the ground, chest flat, chin digging. The rid in midstream did not slide from the horse. Others close in about him and in minutes all splashed out of the water on the far side. Latigo heard the throb of hooves di away in distance. The river calmed, sheathed in moonligh again. There was no more shouting. The silence was sud den and close.

He lay on his back, shoulders hard against dry groun and gulped air, rifle across his chest, till his body coole. When there was no more sweat on his forehead or unde his arms he walked to the river and doused his head. Water coursed his skin when he straightened. He picked up the Winchester, looked for and found the Colt and walked back to the house.

The water trough had been ripped asunder. The pump had been uprooted. He didn't touch either. Corral fence posts leaned askew or lay flat on the ground. He put fingers in his mouth and whistled and heard the gelding whinny in response. In a minute the bay trotted out of shaded moonlight. He straightened posts and replaced rails.

He went back to the house, closed the door and lay on the bed, body-tired, staring through the dark to the ceiling he couldn't see.

They hadn't wasted any time.

"Maybe they were Indians," said the sheriff. "Lots of Apache braves running loose around here."

"They weren't Apaches, Sheriff," said Latigo.

"How do you know? See any of them?"

"I saw them. Indians don't make that kind of noise. They tore down my corral. They broke a lot of window glass and they ran off. Apaches wouldn't act like that."

"Why not?"

"An Indian comes when he wants something. When he wants something he asks first. He only starts to fight when you say no. And he fights till he's dead or you are."

"The fact is," said the sheriff. "You don't know who it was."

"I know who I think it was."

"That's not the same thing, mister!"

"I winged one of them."

"That wouldn't tell me anything. Cowhands get gun-

32

shot wounds all the time. Some of the men around here play rough. Maybe it was a welcome home party."

Latigo stared, angry. "That's right, Sheriff," he said. "It could have been, but for one thing. Nobody but you, the clerk in the land office and Ed Harrison knew I was home."

"What's that supposed to mean?"

"Ed Harrison and the land clerk I trust."

The sheriff wasn't roused by the insult as he should have been. Latigo found the man's eyes uncertain. "Maybe this is not such a good town, mister," said the man with the star on his shirt. "Maybe Gila Bend doesn't suit you." Latigo did not speak. The sheriff gestured and went on. "You could do a lot worse than to move on."

"I just got here, Sheriff."

"You could ride some more. You're used to the back of a horse. You're young . . . got a lot to live for."

"Don't think so, Sheriff," said Latigo. "Native air's always good for what ails a man. I think I'll go see Kincaid."

The sheriff looked up quickly. He did not speak. Latigo regarded the man at the desk. "Sheriff," he said calmly. "The way I see it, a man's got a right to defend himself. No law in the world would deny that. How he does it depends on the man. He can wait for the danger to come right up to him before he draws his gun. Or, if he knows where the danger is coming from, he can ride a way out to meet it. Fact is, he's entitled to shoot the other fellow wherever he finds him."

"Not if the other fellow doesn't have a gun in his hand!"

"He had a gun in his hand last night!"

"You don't know who it was last night."

"Sheriff," said Latigo evenly. "I'll shoot anybody I think aims to shoot me. I'd even shoot you. . . !"

The lawman blustered, red-faced. "Now, look here, young fellow!"

"Stop talking, Sheriff. You know who it was!"

Outside the sheriff's office a six-foot tall, eighteen year man sat on a horse in the sunlight waiting for Latigo Lansen to come out. He didn't look anywhere but at the jail door and when Latigo appeared the rider shifted in the saddle, straightened his back and wet his lips. "Hi! Mister Lansen," he said.

33

Latigo recognised the yellow hair and brown-skinned bony face from days ago. Buck wasn't arguing or pleading with his father now, not spitting-mad-honest-to-God angry; he sat on a fine looking blue roan horse hoping to be told to get off.

"I'm Buck . . . Buck Hemingway," the youth said quickly because Latigo was staring and hadn't made any sign. "We talked . . . days ago when you rode by our place. Remember?"

Latigo stepped nearer the horse. "I remember. What're you doing here?"

"Wanted to see you, Mister Lansen. Wanted to talk to you. It's right important, if you'd spare me but a minute."

"Where are your folks, Buck?"

"They went on. They . . . Ma and Pa both . . . said it was all right for me to come see you."

"Me?"

"Yes, sir. You."

Latigo breathed. "Get off your horse, Buck. We can't talk like this, you on a horse and me on the ground."

Buck stepped down and stood level, even better looking now because he wore a hat. "Didn't want to get down . . . in case you said no."

"No to what?"

Buck Hemingway was hesitant about it, slow to start and then, when he did begin after a chestful of air, talking in a rush of words that left him breathless. "That day you came by, Mister Lansen, you talked to Pa. I heard you say you owned some land around here. Pa said they'd have you off it in no time at all but you said maybe not. The way you said it sounded to me like you didn't intend to be run off your land. Seemed to me like you were of a mind to hold on good to what was yours." He stopped to fill his lungs for more.

"That's right, Buck."

The boy nodded quickly. "Well, sir, what I wanted to see you about was . . . could I work for you, Mister Lansen?" The sun was bright on his troubled face, light flooded his forehead and parted lips. "I know all about ranch work. Pa taught me everything. I can break a horse or throw a steer. Can do anything Pa does. He said so."

"He knows you're here?"

"Yes, sir. He knows."

34

"Why do you want to work for me, Buck?"

Buck wound rein thong about his hand and blinked in the sun. "I don't want to leave here. That's the honest truth. I just don't want to go."

"But you can't walk away from your folks just like that, Buck."

"A man's got to walk away sometime, Mister Lansen. If he's a grown man."

Latigo tried to think of reasons why the idea wasn't good. "Buck," he said. "I'm on my own. My money's in Phoenix right now buying stock. I can't afford to hire help."

"You don't have to pay me. I'll work for nothing, excepting my keep."

"You weren't thinking of Kincaid, were you?"

Buck was honest. He didn't look away. Latigo respected him for it. "Couldn't not think about him," said the big-framed youth. "Reckon there's nothing I could do, anyway, even if he did run us off. He's got a bill of sale with Pa's name on it."

It was a hard thing to say no. Latigo found it impossible. The boy was anxious and the refusal would mean more to him than to the man who made it. Besides, Buck was eighteen years old; life is just starting to mean something then, and that's when it hurts most. He studied the boy's strong shining features. "All right," he said slowly. "You can stay."

Buck's chest swelled. Worry and doubt drained out of his face. His eyes brightened. "Thanks, Mister Lansen," he said. "I won't give you cause to regret it."

Latigo nodded. "Since I'm not paying you money," he said. "You'd better forget the Mister part. My given name's Latimer but people close to me call me Latigo."

The grin spread all over Buck's face. "Latigo? That's a good name for a man, Mister Lansen. Latigo sounds fine!"

"First thing you do, Buck, is call with Ed Harrison. Tell him I sent you. Get yourself a parcel of nails and a cross-cut saw. Second thing you do is ride out to the ranch, mend the water butt and set up the pump."

"Yes, sir. I sure will."

"You know how to get there?"

"I'll find it."

"It's south. Stay on this side of the river. Fix the corral fence while you're in a fixing frame of mind."

"Sure. Anything else?"

Buck stepped into the saddle. Latigo looked up, was slow for a minute, then said it. "You're not wearing a gun, Buck."

The boy's face flushed under the sunburn. "Pa didn't take too kindly to side arms, Mister Lansen," he said. "That's the only reason I'm not wearing a gunbelt."

"Ed Harrison will fix you up. Get going now and do what I told you."

"Yes, sir."

Latigo mounted and tipped his hat forward to shade his eyes. He walked the horse south and after a while crossed the river. Buck watched him out of sight, wheeled the roan and made for the store feeling taller than a pine tree and stronger than he had any right to be.

He walked straight to the glass-topped counter at the back of the store where Harrison displayed guns. A dozen pistols lay under the glass, shiny and new and clean. "All right if I look at a gun, Mister Harrison?"

"Sure, son. Go ahead."

Buck slid back the glass and lifted out a Colt. He'd never owned a gun before. There were rifles in the house, used for hunting prairie dogs, coyote or maybe a prong-buck, though it was rare to get close enough to the gazelle to even sight your gun; or when you were trail-herding cattle north. There'd been six-guns, too, and he knew how to handle a pistol but his father had never actually made the gesture of saying that any one of them was his to keep.

He held the Colt up to the light, using both hands, closed an eye and turned his body in a circle, taking in the shelves and walls and merchandise of the store through an empty chamber barrel. Ed Harrison's long face became enclosed and enlarged in the tight round frame. So did the dark-haired girl Buck hadn't seen when he strode into the store.

The chamber barrel framed her face and shut out everything else around her. She didn't take her eyes from him and she didn't smile. He regarded her for nearly a minute from behind the gun until he realised that the

36

reason she didn't smile or move was because she was frightened. He lowered the gun quickly.

"It's not loaded, ma'am," he said at once. He touched his hat and nodded. "Didn't mean to frighten you."

She didn't speak and still her lips did not move. Her face was calm and small and her clear eyes thoughtful. There was no reproof. She regarded him for long deep moments and he didn't dare move away from the gentle penetration of two glistening brown eyes that both unnerved him and introduced him to a new kind of wonder. He became aware of himself for the first time. He knew he had arms and legs and shoulders and wore pants.

His face heated up like a branding iron. He turned back to the gun case wishing there had been a mirror on the wall somewhere so that he could have seen her without her knowing that he did. She picked up her parcel and left. He turned quickly when she reached the door but she did not look back.

Ed Harrison's voice boomed.

"Aiming to buy yourself a Colt, son?"

"It's to go on Mister Lansen's bill," Buck said quickly. "He said for me to tell you. I want a gunbelt, too, and a cross-cut saw and four-inch nails."

"Sure, boy. Won't take but a minute. Pick yourself a gunbelt. Mister Lansen fancied one of the light coloured ones. Gunbelt sure improves a man. He looked good walking out of here."

Buck selected a yellow belt, new and stiff, heavy with the smell of unworn leather. "You mean one of these?"

"The very same!"

"This'll do for me, too."

He buckled the belt and holstered the gun. It added weight and years and experience. Harrison nodded approval and set a box of shells by the cross-cut saw. Buck stared at the storekeeper.

"Who was that, Mister Harrison? What's her name?"

Harrison's lips puckered. He shook his head. "That would be cheating, boy," he said. "Fine looking young fellow like you doesn't need any help. When I was a young buck, same as you, I just went right up to a pretty girl and spoke my piece."

"Maybe she'd be mad at me ... or something. I mean for speaking right out."

37

"Reckon not, boy. That's the way it's got to be done."

Buck grabbed the parcel of nails and the saw. Harrison spoke again.

"Go easy with the nails, son. They're sixty cents a pound right now."

At the door Buck looked both ways and it wasn't until he straddled the horse that he saw her walking towards the white painted church. He turned the roan and followed. She was stepping from the boardwalk to cross the street by the bank when he reached her. She waited. He slid from the saddle. Her face was sunlit.

" 'Day, ma'am," he said. "Hope you won't get mad at me for speaking. I'm . . . Buck Hemingway, ma'am . . ."

She didn't mind being spoken to. This time she smiled. "That's nice," she said, her voice pleased and gentle. "I'm Rebecca Nevin."

"Howdy, ma'am."

He tipped his hat again. She went on then and he didn't follow. She passed out of sight behind the church and he climbed back on the horse. Ed Harrison was standing by the door of his store when Buck rode by. "You do like I said, boy?" he called out.

Buck nodded. "Yes, sir. I did."

"Good man!"

Buck rode south to look for the stone markers of the Lansen land. The sky was high and clear and there was a wind in the air.

Kincaid didn't leave any doubt in anybody's mind. The markers were built of stone, two feet thick, seven feet high and topped by a pair of longhorns. The granite squarestone set into the pillar bore the name KINCAID.

Latigo eased the gelding down to the river and rode close to the water. The land on the other side was his, the river a boundary. When he rode again to higher ground he skirted grazing cattle. The sun was high, the air warm. The cattle moved hardly at all. Blue and purple mountains reached out of distance for the sky. Until he heard the beat of hooves the only sound had been the bellow of a wandering steer.

Two horsemen rode close with a jangle of bit.

"Where you heading, mister?"

"Kincaid."

38

Latigo didn't recognise either the men or the horses. Last night dust had clung to their faces, had filled the air.

"You got business up at the house?"

"Wouldn't be riding otherwise."

"What kind of business, mister?"

"None of yours."

His gunbelt was new. The two men stared hard at the Colt and at him. "You a stranger around here?" he was asked. He pointed to the land on the other side of the river.

"The name's Lansen. That's my land over there."

"Lansen?" The horsemen exchanged glances. "Reckon we'd better ride a ways with you."

Latigo unholstered the gun. "Ride up front," he directed. "Don't trust people I can't see." The riders wheeled horses and started off ahead of him. "Was that fellow hurt bad last night?" he asked. Both men looked back. Neither spoke. Latigo didn't speak again, either.

The Kincaid house was big and low and stone-built; strong and rooted, with years behind and ahead of it, set like a throne in the empire of cattle land that spread out for miles, running down to the river or to the north or sweeping magnificently south and west. The morning view from any of the wide, curtained western windows of the polished pinewood door was the purple-streaked mountain range rising mistily from yellow valley grass. A wooden verandah ran along the front and on two sides. Ten yards from the varnished door stood two giant saguarro, wild with pink and lavender bloom, heavy with scent.

The great door swung open as Latigo hitched the gelding. The Mexican who appeared was an old man, face straight and lined, lips gentle and aristocratic.

Latigo stood out in sunlight. Behind him. Behind him, near two more ornamental stone pillars topped by shining longhorns, the two riders climbed down and waited. There was no sound at all and he thought there should have been. The corral was empty of saddle horses. Farther back, the bunkhouse door was closed and that, too, was strange. Men ought to have been riding in from the range to eat. Smoke ought to have risen from the cookhouse chimney. Saddles should have been slung on the corral rails and horses sucking at water over by the windmill. There was no movement behind any of the windows of the house and nobody in sight except the manservant and the two horsemen by the pillars.

The slender-faced man came forward from the doorway. Latigo nodded. "I'd like to see Mister Kincaid," he said.

At the edge of the verandah the Mexican bent his head in apology. "I am sorry, Senor. That is not possible."

"I want to see him. Tell him I'm here. The name is Lansen."

"Senor, it is forbidden."

"Why?"

"Senor Kincaid is resting. He is not to be disturbed."

"Is he tired?" asked Latigo. "Was he out riding last night?"

The two men stood away from the longhorn pillars with a click of spurs. Latigo drew his gun and turned. "You two men stay where you are," he ordered. "I'm not overly particular who I shoot."

They stood in bright sunlight, not moving, waiting.

"Tell Mister Kincaid I want to see him," he said again to the Mexican.

"I am sorry, Senor. It is not of my doing. Senor Kincaid must not be disturbed at this hour."

Latigo pointed the gun in the air. The two men behind him moved and stopped short. "Maybe this will wake him up!" he said. He curled a finger about the trigger and heard rapid footsteps. The Mexican stood aside and the woman appeared.

"Don't fire that gun!" she ordered sharply.

She came forward, dressed as before, fingers tight about the riding whip, her hair aflame in sunlight. Latigo did not lower the gun. She walked close, dark eyes bright. "What do you want, Mister Lansen?"

"I want to see your father."

"With a gun in your hand?"

"Yes, ma'am. Every time you see me from now on I'll have a gun in my hand."

"To give you courage?"

"No, ma'am. I'm just playing the kind of cards your father deals."

Colour rushed to her cheeks and she raised her voice. "Gaskin!" she called. The two men near the stone pillars moved. Latigo turned and pointed the gun. Both men

40

hesitated in stride and halted, hands close to gun handles, watching his eyes. Latigo gestured with the Colt.

"Throw them over there."

They did what he ordered. The woman could not command them otherwise. Guns scattered earth as they hit the ground. A dark glitter rose in her eyes. "You'll be sorry for this," she said quietly.

Latigo did not look at her. "Threatening people is a bad habit, ma'am," he said. "Tell your father I want to see him."

"My father is resting," she said. "Why do you want to see him?"

"Want to tell him what happened last night. He already knows about it but . . ."

"Then there's no need to tell him, is there?"

"Yes, ma'am. He's got to know I came to the right place to talk about it."

"Tell me," she said. "I'd like to know."

Latigo faced her. The two men stood as he had ordered, guns on the ground yards away and out of reach. There still wasn't any movement about the house, the bunkhouse door stayed closed. The Mexican stood on the verandah in the shade, his hands clasped.

"I'd be wasting breath," Latigo said deliberately. "You already know."

Crimson flooded her face and he thought it a pity she was such a fine looking woman. The man who broke her down as he would a high-necked filly would have to use the whip and she might never forgive him, even though she wouldn't be a woman until it had been done.

"Are you calling me a liar?" she demanded.

His voice stayed calm and level. "Yes, ma'am. Seems to be a habit around here, like the wearing of guns."

"How dare you come here and . . ."

"I didn't come to make trouble, ma'am," he said. "Expected to deal with the man of the house. If you were a man you'd know that. Came to tell your father that I won't run away from any kind of trouble he tries to make. I'm here to stay. Ten or twelve men came riding round my place last night shooting off guns. They broke a lot of window glass, tore down my corral fence and drove off my horse. If I'd been killed they'd have said it was an accident."

"You have enemies, Mister Lansen," she said.

41

"Yes, ma'am. Can see that. But I reckon I'm not alone. The Kincaids have an enemy, too. Me."

"If I were a man you wouldn't say that!"

"That's right, ma'am. I wouldn't. I'd shoot you."

She was startled. "So what do you propose to do?" she asked. "Seeing that I'm your enemy, a woman and that you can't shoot me."

"Not a thing. You're not the kind of woman I'd take any trouble with."

That stung and her face coloured. This time it wasn't only anger but injured pride as well that flushed her cheeks. But there was doubt. Her fingers tightened on the riding whip. She wanted to beat him and didn't because that wasn't the thing to do. He was a stranger who challenged her on her own ground and she didn't know how to meet the challenge. The sun was on his face and he stood the way a man should who isn't afraid. The day of the fight out on the range she watched him climb on to his horse and ride away without looking back. When he had gone, remembering him, she had studied the face of Joe Erskine riding by her side. Until now she had never been unsure.

"I think you should go," she said quietly.

Latigo slid the gun back into the holster. "I'll go," he said. "Tell your men not to pick up their guns and tell them not to come after me."

Shadow appeared on the ground. Joe Erskine walked into sight from the side of the house. He held a gun in his hand. Latigo turned and saw the newcomer. She didn't speak and she didn't react to the dark-skinned man's presence. Instead, she looked from one face to the other, seeking to discover the name and the nature of the difference.

Erskine stepped forward and motioned to the men standing midway between the saguarro and the stone pillars. "Pick them up," he ordered. The men recovered the guns, moved closer and waited. The gun in Erskine's hand moved. He wore his pants tight about his hips and his waist was flat. "We don't like people giving orders around here," he said. "Especially strangers."

"Joe . . ." she began. The gun waved her to silence. She expected Latigo Lansen to speak and wondered why he didn't. It couldn't be that he was still not afraid. Three

42

men surrounded him, all had guns in their hands, and he had declared himself an enemy. He ought to be afraid and he ought to speak.

"You're the fellow who saw the fight," Erskine said. "When I beat the living daylights out of Ben Nevin."

Latigo nodded. "Ben Nevin walked away from the fight," he said. "You were lying on the ground."

Erskine's hand tightened on the gun. "That's a damned lie, stranger, and you know it!" he shouted.

Again Latigo nodded. The woman watched his face. "All right," he said. "It's a lie. Everybody tells lies. I'll tell you another. I know why you were fighting."

The woman moved, but not quickly enough. Erskine's hand swung and the gun hit the side of Latigo's face and his forehead. The men behind moved closer. She raised a hand and cried out "Joe!" and before Latigo hit the ground he heard her voice very clearly.

The earth rushed up to clutch at him. He was unable to rise because he couldn't see and because of the branding iron somebody held against his face. But sounds came to him, her voice again, from a distance.

"Joe!" sharp and commanding, like a whiplash. "You didn't need to do that!"

"Sure I did. He's a trouble maker. You know what the boss said about him."

"You didn't have to hit him. He was leaving."

"He sure enough won't come back!" The voice laughed and a boot pushed hard on his shoulder. "Get up, mister! Get up and get out!"

Latigo felt the heat of blood on his face. There didn't seem to be any room in his head for thoughts until her voice rushed in again, sudden and knife-edged. "Don't do that! Leave him alone. Let him get up!"

He drew in his knees and raised himself. There was nothing to hold on to and the ground wasn't flat. Getting upright took all of a minute.

From deep inside the shaded house the wide high doorway made a straight-edged frame that shut out everything else except the man rising from the ground, another man with a gun in his hand, and the fair-haired woman. The light outside was strong and the man who stood watching from within saw it all very clearly. He heard what had been said but did not move to take part in what happened in

43

front of his house. The man with the gun was his foreman. The woman was his daughter and the man who had been hit with the flat of the six-gun was Latimer Lansen, his enemy.

It was the first time Matthew Kincaid had seen Latigo.

Joe Erskine didn't holster the gun. He stood back while Latigo rose and scooped up his hat. The woman watched without speaking. Latigo looked away from them both, walked to his horse and stepped into the saddle. Erskine followed his movements, dark face creased in the light, gun at his side. The other men eased away. Latigo walked the gelding between the stone pillars and Hildy Kincaid wanted him to look back, wanted him to turn and say something.

"You didn't have to do that, Joe," she said when Latigo was out of sight.

"Sure I did, Hildy. He's got to be taught a lesson. He's a trouble maker."

"If he's a trouble maker, he hasn't finished. It might be that he hasn't started."

"I can take care of him."

She regarded his dark, sunlighted face and depthless eyes. His lips were parted and he was pleased with himself. Questioning thoughts rushed across her mind and before she spoke his look had become puzzled and hurt. His lips straightened and he slid the gun back into the holster to escape her speculation.

"Why were you fighting, Joe? You and Ben Nevin?"

The man inside the house heard the question and listened for the answer.

"Nothing!" lied Erskine. "He called me a dirty name. That's all!"

Erskine moved away and the woman alone was framed by the doorway. She walked slowly into the house without closing the door until she was greater than the frame and the door hidden behind her approaching figure. She halted when she saw her father. Matthew Kincaid raised himself from the edge of the table. "That was Lansen," he said.

She agreed. "He came to see you about what happened last night."

"What was that?"

"Some men shot up his house, broke down his corral fences and drove off his horse."

44

"Is that why Huggins has a bullet hole in his shoulder?"

"I suppose so, father."

Her eyes were on his face but her thoughts were with the man on the gelding. Matthew Kincaid noted the distance between his daughter and himself. "Hildy," he said. "I didn't tell Joe to do that. Last night, I mean."

She came back to him. "It's what was done before, father," she said. "He thought it had to be done again. This time I'm not so sure."

"Wait and see, girl."

"I'll wait but maybe I won't want to see. He's not afraid of you and that makes a difference. His anger doesn't have to be defensive."

"He wouldn't dare!"

"You wait and see," she said.

Matthew Kincaid watched his daughter all the way upstairs.

CHAPTER FOUR

"WHAT'D you walk into, Latigo . . . side of a barn?"

Blood marked the side of his face, a bruise on his forehead had begun to darken and there was a swelling. He sorted out two red workshirts and set them by a box of shells. "The side of a gun," he said. "I want these and these."

"It was in somebody's hand, I reckon."

"Joe Erskine's."

The storekeeper did not show any surprise. "Where'd you run into him?"

"Kincaid's."

"Why'd you go there?"

"The sheriff wouldn't so I figured I'd better."

"That's no reason. You'd be doing better to stay away from there."

To Latigo's way of thinking that wasn't good advice. If the Kincaids weren't told, they wouldn't know. And it was only fair to tell a man that you were his enemy. He thought about it for moments. "Part of the price a man pays for having rights is defending them," he said. "Otherwise he's got no reason to stay alive. Staying alive is my

45

chief aim. On the way here I killed an Indian to prove it. I've done some fighting and I know how."

"Kincaid's a big man, young fellow."

"He stands on two feet, same as the rest of us. The only thing big about Kincaid is the amount of ground he owns."

"And that's power, boy, power! Out here land is money and power. He's too big for one man to fight!"

"There's only one man left. Me!"

Ed Harrison glared and made allowance for the bloody face and the marks of the gun. "That kind of talk comes from a fool or a brave man," he said with a snort. "I don't reckon you're anybody's fool, but you're sure enough not talking sense!"

"I stand on two feet like he does," declared Latigo. "But what I'm standing on is my own. Nobody's taking it from me!"

"Has he tried to do that?"

"Last night," said Latigo and remembered the breaking glass and the sting of cuts on his shoulders when he rolled on the floor. "They came riding and shooting."

"So you're buying bullets!"

"It's his language. I didn't come here to make trouble. Came to start living. I'm twenty-six years old and it's time I picked out my ground."

Harrison slapped a broad palm on the counter. "Dammit, man, it doesn't have to be here!" he stated sharply. "There's plenty of land. Anywhere you look there's virgin land waiting to be bought. Ten cents an acre is all it costs. You're twenty-six years old! You think this land is better than anywhere else? You think it's worth getting killed for?"

"What do you want me to do . . . sell it to Kincaid?"

"Why not? There'd be no shame in that!"

Latigo looked squarely at the storekeeper, a big man, shouting at him for his own good. "Are you a coward, Mister Harrison?" he asked calmly.

Harrison bristled. His eyebrows rose sharply and came down low. "I'm damned if I'm a coward, Mister Lansen!" he declared hotly. "Never ran away from anything in my life and if I was thirty years younger you wouldn't say that!"

"That's what I mean," said Latigo in the same voice.

"I'd be more than ashamed to run away from what's my own."

The storekeeper glared. "Guess you think you're smart, don't you? Getting me all riled up just to prove me wrong!"

"Had to tell you how I feel. It's my land. I was born on it. It's got Lansen blood on it. My mother is buried in it."

"Every inch of this territory's got blood on it, boy. Indian blood, white man's blood. If you think Kincaid cares about that, you're wrong. He's not that kind of man." The storekeeper paused, quieted and squinted at Latigo. "If you're going to fight him for what's yours, you'll need help. Not much good with a gun myself but if there's anything you want done, you say it."

"Aren't you mad at me?"

"Looks and feelings might be different. If you were older you'd know that. Maybe I could round up some men I know."

"It's not a war."

"Defence is part of fighting, too, isn't it?"

"I've got help, thanks. Young Buck Hemingway is riding with me."

"He's only a boy. You need men."

"He's the size of a man. And he's got good reasons."

Harrison wrapped the shirts carelessly, angrily, eyes glaring. "You sure enough get the better of me every time, don't you?" he complained. "You'd think a young fellow like you'd have better manners. I'm older than you, boy! Why don't you want help? You can't do it all by yourself!"

Latigo hadn't come to start a war. He'd come to stand on his own ground and everything that had to be done had to be done by him. "Living's a thing a man has to do for himself," he said. "What he does is what he thinks has to be done and unless it's done the way he wants, it might as well not be done at all. When a man stands behind a gun, he's on his own."

Harrison found a hole in that argument and smacked the counter top smartly. "Well, you're wrong there, young fellow!" he said. "A friend can tell him where to point the gun! Besides, people are not in the world by themselves. Something's wrong with a lonely man. He's a crittur! You aim to live in Gila Bend, you better take the hand of friendship when it's held out to you!"

Latigo gathered up the shirts and the box of shells. At the door Harrison spoke again. "Mister Lansen..." he said. Latigo looked back. "You've got blood on your face. Don't look good. Wash it off."

"Soon as I get home."

The telegraph office was at the end of the street by the bank. When Latigo stepped down men stared at his face but no one spoke. He was out of the office again inside a minute. He rounded the bank corner and rode back to the store. "Was expecting a message at the telegraph office," he said at the doorway. "Hasn't come this far yet. Told him to let you have it. Buck will pick it up next time he's in town."

Harrison grinned. "Reckon he'll be in town right often from now on."

"Why?"

"Guess I didn't tell you. He's a man with some sense. Knows more about living than you."

"What'd he do wrong?"

"Not a damn thing. Just found himself a girl, that's all."

Latigo came farther into the store, shirt parcel under his arm. "Buck's eighteen years old," he said.

"He's big enough. Said so yourself!"

"What happened Mister Harrison? I'm responsible for him."

"Was wearing his new gunbelt at the time. Maybe that helped. Took one look, then went after her and spoke his piece, bold as ever you'd see."

"What's her name?"

"Rebecca. Her Pa owns the livery stable...name of Nevin."

Latigo rode by his side of the river, waded the gelding into the water and waited while it slaked its thirst. The land on both sides looked fine, wind from the range warm and clear and filling a cloudless sky. Perfection in natural things made a man lonely, and he was lonely for he needed more than he possessed. Without a woman at his side, on a horse or walking out of the door of the house when he rode home, he still wasn't living. That was what he had come here to do, live; to put down his roots, work the land, raise cattle, feel his own ground underfoot when he walked or rode a horse, to watch the western sky at night when it spouted torrents of flame, and then to turn his back on it and close the pinewood door behind him while window glass glinted red.

But he was twenty-six years old and cattle weren't all that had to be raised in a growing country. Roots belonged to the body. Owning land wasn't all and it wasn't enough. A woman gave a man cause to fight and gave him courage, too. Years spent on a horse, facing the wind, made him aware of his body, made him strong.

So far she didn't look like the kind of woman he had in mind. There was hardly anything in the world as bad as a stiff-necked woman who thought more of her pride than she did of living, being a woman and doing womanly things.

With a colt there are ways of doing it. First you put a hackamore bit in its mouth, a saddle on its back and you straddle it and stay straddled till it stops bucking and fighting the rein, till silky flanks quiver and tremble like wind-kissed deep water and flaring nostrils reach for your hand. When it knows who is master you can be nice to it. You pet it and brush it down and feed it grain. You work your hands all over it till it knows not to be afraid. You whistle and it comes running, glad to be near you, willing to belong to you.

But what do you do with a woman who carries a whip, walks with the stretching gait of a male stripling, stands up to any man she sees and likely as not lets him feel the weight of the whip? How do you tame her, supposing all the time that after you had done the taming, she was the kind of woman you wanted?

Buck hadn't experienced any trouble. He'd just walked up to the girl of his choice and said what was in his mind. And Buck was eighteen years old.

The gelding made rings in the water. It was time to go. He turned the animal and rode out of the water. Yellow grass swept away from both banks and her name kept coming into his head.

Buck dropped the hammer and came running. "Hi! Latigo. I did what you said." Latigo stepped down by the filled water trough and dropped his hat. Buck stared. "What happened? You fall off your horse, Latigo?"

"Pistol whipped," said Latigo.

"Who did it?" Buck demanded. "You going after him?"

Latigo tugged the shirt from his back and bent his head

49

to the water. "Not right now," he said. "He'll keep." The water was cold and eased the ache. Halfway to the door of the house he turned. "Hear you met a girl in town."

Buck whirled, dismayed and curious. "Huh?"

"What'd you say to her?"

"Said my name, that's all."

When Latigo had spoken to Hildy Kincaid she'd carried a riding crop in her hand, had just whipped one man and was itching to whip another. He hadn't been civil or polite. He doubted if he'd touched his hat and he was sure he hadn't said his name. "She talk back to you?" he asked.

"Yes, sir. She did the same as me. Said her name. I guess it was all right for me to talk right out the way I did, else she wouldn't have said her name, would she?"

"Guess not. You planning to get married, Buck?"

Buck's jaw dropped. "Married?" he yelled. "Latigo! I'm eighteen years old!"

"You're big enough."

Buck looked down at himself, all the way down the front of his faded pants to his boots. "You mean I did wrong, Latigo?"

Latigo dried his chest with the rolled-up shirt. "You did real well," he agreed.

Buck laughed in relief. "You were only fooling, Latigo."

"Not fooling now, Buck. When you go see Rebecca, watch out for Joe Erskine."

"He's Kincaid's man. I know about him. What's he got to do with her?"

"Not a thing except that he doesn't want anybody else to come near her."

"I'm not scared of him, Latigo. Besides, she answered me back, didn't cut me off or anything. That doesn't look like she belonged to him."

"She doesn't. He wants her to. And I know you're not scared, but he's been using a gun for a long time."

"I know how to use a gun," Buck claimed. "I just never owned one. Look." He whipped the Colt from the holster smoothly and quickly, his hand steady, belly tightened and knees just bent. Latigo was impressed. Buck looked well, belonged to the plains and the back of a horse. "Wanted to kill Erskine for what he did to us," he said seriously.

Latigo thought the notion dangerous. "That's the

50

trouble with life, Buck," he said. "A fellow never gets to kill all the people he wants."

Buck didn't laugh. Minutes later, when Latigo was pushing head and arms into a new red workshirt inside the house, the boy's voice called out sharply. "Latigo!" He backed to the door of the ranch house and pointed. "Some men riding this way."

There were seven of them riding by the river bank, on his side, coming in a hurry; six riders about a square-shouldered man who sat erect in the saddle. They swept up from the bank, disappeared for moments and then came abreast on the draw. When they slowed dust fell away.

Latigo waited till he recognised Kincaid on the middle horse. "Go inside, Buck," he said.

Buck turned his gaze from the approaching horsemen. "There going to be a fight, Latigo?"

"Shouldn't be."

"I can use a gun, Latigo. Let me stay out here with you."

"You can use it better from the house. Cover me in case they start anything."

"Yes, sir."

Latigo reached for the Winchester, jacked a bullet into place and strode out into the light. He was beside the Indian lance when the seven men reined and halted. For a minute there was near silence. He held the gun across his middle and waited. From behind he heard the click as Buck thumbed back the hammer of his Colt.

None of the riders dismounted. The horses were quiet. Kincaid's hard blue eyes stared out from under the shade of his wide-brimmed hat. He rode a fine looking square-chested sorrel. "You're Lansen," he said.

"I'm Lansen."

Kincaid saw the house and the corral fence, the pump, repaired water butt and the Indian lance. The windbreak behind the house was silent. He came back to the man with the rifle. "Know who I am?"

"Reckon I do."

"You own all this land?"

"It's mine."

"You got a deed for it . . . a land grant certificate?"

"It's registered at the land office. John Mallow will show you the entry any time you like."

"Taxes paid?"

"I don't owe anybody anything. Especially the government."

Kincaid's face did not change. "Since you own it all and it's clear, there's no reason why you can't sell."

"One reason I know of."

"Name it."

"Don't want to."

"That's no reason. Name your price, Lansen."

"It's got no price. You can't buy it."

"You'll sell."

"Don't try and make me, Mister Kincaid."

"I'm here to talk business, Lansen," said Kincaid. He clasped hands about the saddle horn and heaved his body forward to get down.

Latigo brought the rifle up across his belly. "Mister Kincaid," he said. "This is my land and you're trespassing. Get off that horse and I'll kill you."

Kincaid sat still, face tight, eyes alight. Like his daughter, thought Latigo, everything comes out in the eyes; anger, surprise and bafflement. "What're you talking about, Lansen?" demanded the rancher. "I came here to do business!"

"The land's not for sale."

Kincaid stared down at him. None of the other men moved at all. Joe Erskine sat on the right of the landowner, eyes fixed on the man with the rifle. "You talk like a brave man, Lansen," said Kincaid. "But only a fool does that. I'm going to own this land . . . if necessary over your dead body!"

Latigo brought the rifle up high, glad to know that Buck was behind him in the house with a cocked six-gun in his hand. "Land wouldn't do you much good if you were dead, Mister Kincaid," he said. "You'll never own this."

He should have seen what was coming and didn't. Afterwards he still didn't think they would have tried it. It was too open. Buck stopped it halfway and prevented murder.

Latigo stood to one side of the Indian lance, rifle in his hands and light across his face. The men on horses looked bigger than they were. Kincaid stared down at him and then only half glanced to the side, so quickly that there was

52

almost no movement at all. And Erskine didn't react to a signal.

"Fool's talk!" exclaimed Kincaid. "Like fool's gold! Looks well, shines up nice, sounds good, but it's nothing . . . just nothing! You're a fool, Lansen, and you're talking yourself into a parcel of trouble. I own the whole of this valley!"

"You don't own the Lansen land."

"Not yet, but I reckon I will," predicted Kincaid and looked at the Apache lance piercing the earth. "What's that thing?"

This was when it happened, when he should have known and expected deceit. The lance was private and precious to him. He moved his eyes to look at the relic and everything happened too quickly for him to know about until it was over.

The moment Latigo's eyes left Kincaid, Joe Erskine's hand moved. The gun hadn't risen high enough to be used when the explosion of a Colt smote the air with a hard round thunderclap, sudden and short. Erskine convulsed in the saddle and held his wrist. The gun leaped from his hand and hit the dust and the horses started up as he cried out. Hands that had begun reaching for guns halted halfway. Surprise lighted the faces of six of the men on horses. Hurt and anger showed on Erskine's as blood seeped about his fingers. Kincaid stared straight ahead.

"It's an Apache lance," said Latigo and hope that Buck would not come out of the house. "And I wouldn't try anything like that a second time. You'll die first, Mister Kincaid."

"Joe's a fool," said Kincaid. "I didn't know he'd try anything. Who've you got in there?"

"What you haven't got. A friend."

The rancher glared. "All right, Lansen," he said. "I know you can fight. You've been in the war. I know all about you!"

"I didn't start the fight."

"You're making a fight necessary. Supposing we talk business. I'm bigger than you, I'll last longer. I want your land!"

"What for?"

There was no answer to that. There could only be bluster. The question had never before been asked. "Be-

53

cause it's in my way!" exclaimed Kincaid. "I own the rest of the valley and you're a thorn. I want my cattle all over here!"

"You already own more land than any one man could ever need, Mister Kincaid," said Latigo. He shifted the gun, eased himself. "Would you like me to tell you why you want more?"

The rancher glared down. The barrel of the Winchester glinted bright and close. He tried to be amused but none of it was funny. This morning his daughter had acted and spoken strangely. What she meant was that this man was different. He wiped his lips roughly with the heel of his thumb. "All right, Mister Lansen," he said. "Tell me!"

Latigo held the rifle lower. "You're an old man," he said loudly. The other men listened and Buck heard, too. Kincaid stiffened. "Land is like life to you and you're afraid to let go. You're afraid you're going to die, Mister Kincaid. You're even foolish enough to think that the more land you own the longer you'll live. People like me know you can't buy living time or stay longer than your due. Old people like you don't believe it."

There was a full minute's silence. Kincaid stared. He hadn't expected this. The sound of Latigo Lansen's voice was like a blow on the face. Not that what the man standing on the ground said was true. The idea was new to him. He wanted land simply because he wanted land and there didn't have to be a reason, except his daughter Hildy, the best reason of all. You could laugh at a thing like this; fact was, laughter and contempt seemed the best answer if there had been the slightest grain of truth in it. And there wasn't! It was fancy talk, that's all! Fancy talk from a fellow who didn't know enough to keep his mouth shut.

Kincaid looked down at Latigo Lansen, standing with a Winchester rifle held across his middle, his face creased now in the light but a clear face with no age on it, the hard-skinned healthy face of a young man.

Five of the men heard what Latigo said and didn't think about it. Men are hired for their skill on a horse or with a gun, never because they were men and entitled to more. But Joe Erskine had other things on his mind. For one, his hand hurt; second, he hadn't given thought to the fact that Kincaid would die and that was a stupid thing to forget. Everybody dies. It was just that Latigo Lansen was

54

the first man Erskine knew who brought Kincaid down to the level of every other walking man. And that changed things.

He thought of Hildy Kincaid, an uppity woman who claimed and commanded him yet kept him at arm's length. He wondered how big Gila river valley was and what it would be like to be the man who owned it.

Kincaid did the first thing he thought of. He laughed. "We'll see if you act as big as you talk, Lansen!" he said and turned the horse. "Come on, men. I've talked too long to a fool!"

Latigo watched them down the draw. In minutes all seven had splashed across the river and swept steeply up the far bank. Buck came out of the house with the gun in his hand. Admiration filled his eyes. "You sure told him, Latigo," he said. "You sure enough did. I never heard that kind of talk before. He looked all shook up. Why'd you stop, Latigo? I could have listened to more."

Latigo regarded the yellow-headed young giant of a boy before him. "Only said what I thought," he said.

"Guess when you hit a nail it stays drove, Latigo."

"Maybe. I've got something to say to you, Buck."

The tone was different. Buck's face fell. "Did I do wrong, Latigo?"

Latigo shook his head. "You didn't do wrong, Buck. You saved my life. Just wanted to tell you . . . you're a bigger man than I thought."

"Huh . . . ?"

CHAPTER FIVE

For days the mornings were calm, the nights at rest. Buck had to be shown the land. They rode north, south and east and when a Lansen marker stood up out of the ground they reined and appraised the range. In the east the land was high and there was a wind. Buck thought of days that were past and wound rein leather about his fingers. "Sure wish I had my banjo, Latigo."

"Didn't know you were a musical man, Buck."

"Pa brought me one from Phoenix. I can play real good."

"What would you play now, right this minute?"

Buck shrugged, listening to the music in his head. "Don't know. Some kind of horse-riding song, maybe. Something that'd help a fellow along." The horses skirted chaparral without being reined. "You in the war, Latigo?"

"Sure. Was nearly over by the time I got in."

"Do any fighting?"

"Some. Fought at Vicksburg."

"You ever see Mister Lincoln. I mean, plain . . . ?"

"Could have touched him. Heard him speak his speech."

"What was he like, Latigo?"

"Nice, tired old man. Looked like God to me."

Buck looked up, a sudden illuminating thought lighting his whole countenance. "You know what I'd play, Latigo? If I had my banjo, you know what I'd play?"

Latigo nodded. "Sure. You'd play 'Dixie'."

Buck's mouth opened. "How'd you know, Latigo?" he queried. Latigo rode on ahead. Buck spurred the roan and joined up. He held his hat far out over his forehead to shade his eyes and it was the yellow-haired Buck, not Latigo, who voiced pride in the range. "You got nice land here, Latigo," he said. "You got everything a man could ever want."

"You think so?"

"I'm looking at it. Never saw a prettier stretch of ground in my whole life. Used to think the Hemingway dirt was the best but this sure beats all to kingdom come. You got trees for shade and you've got half the river. Don't see what else you could want."

They walked the horses on yellow grass that bent in the wind.

"Want something for myself," Latigo said.

Buck watched the side of Latigo's face. "Something that's not here?"

"Might be here."

"What I can see is land and grass, trees and water. All a man needs."

"He needs more, Buck. Needs a reason for all you can see."

"You own it, don't you? What more reason than that?"

The horses edged sideways down the sandy wall of a

56

wide arroyo, a dry-wash that was like a wound, blood-red with poppy, streaked by wild pea, scabbed by shad scale. They climbed again. "Used to ride on my own a lot," explained Latigo. The horses rose into unbroken sunlight. "Used to talk to myself. Had to do it because I needed to hear a human voice. After a while I got tired doing that because what I was listening to was always the same thing, my own voice. It's nice to own land—land like this that's as near perfect as ever you'll get for Arizona—but it doesn't talk back to you. That's what a man needs most of all."

Buck thought about it. "You mean a woman, don't you, Latigo?"

"That's right."

"Why don't you?"

"Only been here days."

"I mean before this. Before you came back."

"Would have been the wrong thing to do, Buck. Have to find a woman close to my land. If I'd picked a girl somewhere else, I might never have come back. This is my home. Coming here is something I had to do."

"You got your eye on somebody, Latigo?"

"Maybe. Don't reckon anything'll come of it, though."

"Why not? You've got everything a man should have . . . this land and all."

"I might be the wrong man."

Buck thought again, for as long as it took to breast another smooth rise. "You know what you want to do, Latigo?"

Latigo laughed and remembered. "Sure. Go right up to her and speak my piece. Like you!"

"I'm serious, Latigo," insisted Buck. "We didn't get to church much, seeing as how we lived so far from town. But, times, the preacher would come riding by and he'd visit with us for a day and a night. They were nice times, Latigo. He used to tell us all the doings for miles around. Sometimes I didn't want to go to bed, the talk was so good."

"So?"

"That's the man you want to see. He knows everybody and everything. He'll tell you where there's a woman for you. All you have to do is ask him. And it'd be private, too. Nobody would know about it except you and him."

"That what you did, Buck?"

Buck laughed and wheeled the horse. They headed south. It was a day for feeling good and owning the world. They rode home tired and hungry.

Buck was the early riser. In the morning he walked on bare feet to the window to look at the day. He stood in shirt tails and stared, hairs on his calves stiffening. "Latigo!" he said. "Quick!"

"What is it?"

"We've got visitors!"

A hundred yards from the house three straight-backed Apache Indians sat astride paint ponies. Morning light shone on brown-skinned shoulders and thighs. The Indians waited, without motion, without speech.

"What do they want, Latigo? Are they peaceable?"

"Reckon so. They don't look fierce. Guess they want something. That means they won't move till we go out and talk."

The Apaches carried no weapons that Latigo could see. An eagle feather fluttered from the back of each man's head. They faced the house and were patient.

"Put your pants on, Buck. It's all right for an Indian to be naked, but not a white man."

"You going to talk to them?"

"I'll talk. You stay indoors till I call. Don't touch a gun till they start acting up."

Latigo opened the door and stepped away from the house. Buck ran back to the bed and pushed long legs into pants. Latigo walked slowly from the shade of the house, hands by his sides, unarmed, the sun behind and his shadow on the ground. The Indians watched, not moving.

He halted ten yards from the three men riding bareback on slender-legged ponies and made the traditional open-palmed gesture of friendship. His hand movements embraced the earth and the sun and the sky. They were his possessions but the Indians were welcome to share. He touched his lips and invited the Apache to speak.

The tall Indian in the middle pointed to the morning sun as Latigo had done, to the sky and the ground, then to Latigo himself. It was a good sign. The earth was for all men. There would be peace. He did not dismount and his back remained stiff and straight.

The Red man and the eagle have this much in common;

58

both belong to America, both possess strength and a ferocity of pride that makes pain easy to bear. While the eagle crested the skies in feathered glory these sons of the Mimbrenos owned the plains, the rivers and the bison; they knew the sun, the sky, the rain and bitter wind and they, too, experienced the same tugging hope that comes when migrant geese arrow a painted sky. They would never forget that they had been first on this ground and that their great chiefs still rode in silent majesty across heavens gilded by morning light, painted red as the sun went down. For them blood meant victory and vengeance a burning ecstasy. Latigo Lansen acknowledged that pride.

The Apache spoke slowly, haltingly, in short sentences with hand gestures to fill places where there were no words. "Peace treaty is made," he said. "Peace is all land . . ."

Latigo nodded. "Cochise?" he asked.

The Apache pointed to the sky. "Cochise great chief. Father of Apache nation. Smoke peace pipe with white man. No more war."

Latigo displayed his pleasure. The Indian touched his own naked chest. "Apache Running Horse," he announced. Latigo nodded. The Indian indicated the brave on his left. "Apache Barking Dog." Again Latigo nodded. The Indian pointed to his right. "Apache Eagle Feather."

Latigo tapped his own chest. "White Eye Latigo Lansen," he said. The Indians exchanged glances of pleasure. Latigo called out to the man in the house. "Buck!" he cried.

Buck emerged and walked on bare feet. The Indians watched silently as he approached and stared at his yellow hair. When he stood close Latigo laid a hand on the youth's shoulder. "White Eye Leaping Buck," he said.

"Leaping Buck," repeated the Apache, intrigued by the name and the shock of uncombed yellow hair. He was pleased. "Running Horse brings gift," he announced and proffered a rolled animal skin.

"Take it, Buck," said Latigo.

Buck accepted the gift, untied the thongs and unrolled a buffalo skin, glowing rich as redwood in morning light, without knife or arrow mark. Latigo gestured thanks with his hands and spoke it with his lips. "Leaping Buck thanks Apache Running Horse," he said. "He will not forget all men are brothers."

59

The Indian motioned sharply. "Buffalo skin not gift for Leaping Buck," he corrected. "For Latigo Lansen."

Latigo made the thanks his own. Buck straightened. "Go in the house and bring my hunting knife," said Latigo.

Buck had admired the silver handle. "Latigo!" he protested.

"Bring it."

Buck returned with the knife. Latigo held it out, handle towards the Indian. "Gift to Running Horse," he said. "Days of blood are over. No more war."

The Indian took the knife in his hand and inspected it carefully. Latigo waited. The red man nodded, his chest swelled and he regarded the two men on the ground before him. The gift was worthy. He crossed forearms at the wrist. "Apache Running Horse, White Eye Latigo Lansen," he commanded. "Brothers!"

Latigo and Buck watched the Apaches down the draw, across the river and out towards the west to the mountains. "Never talked to an Indian before, Latigo," Buck said. "We won't have any trouble with them, will we?"

"Not if the peace is kept."

"Pa said there used to be a bounty on them right here in Arizona."

"Two hundred and fifty dollars a scalp, Buck," said Latigo.

"The Gila river wasn't always white water. Sometimes it ran red."

Buck rolled the buffalo hide into a bundle. "What're you going to do with it, Latigo?"

"It's yours if you want it."

"What'll I do with it?"

Latigo started back to the house. "I'd give it to my girl, if I had one."

Buck stared after him. "Thanks, Latigo!"

"Get your boots on, boy. We've got things to do."

It didn't happen that day, or the next, or the next. But it had to happen and he rode out across his range looking for it, tempting it, expecting it to ride up to him, expecting to hear a rifle shot from somewhere. Somebody should try to kill him.

He heaved the saddle across the gelding's back.

"Where you going, Latigo?"

60

"Riding. When you're in town call at the Telegraph office. See if there's a message."

"Sure. What kind of message you expecting?"

"The stock should have started south by now. They were to send me word."

"How many coming?"

"Two thousand ... two thousand and some." Latigo stepped into the saddle and swung the gelding round. "Wear your gun, Buck, and look out for who I told you. Don't go near the ravine."

"Sure, Latigo."

He rode off. Buck watched him go and raced for his saddle. He tied the buffalo hide in a tight bundle and set it across his thighs. Last thing he did was spit on his palm and slick back his hair.

Latigo was beyond his own land when he saw the runaway. For a while he had watched Kincaid's cattle on the other side of the river. He listened to the bellows of watering steers and rode on, watching for riders and seeing none. Thunderheads drifted in the west but the sky above him stayed clear. Behind him rose the mountain bastions. The ground fell away in sweeping waves, without the shape or sound of a man on a horse. There was only the wind.

He reined on high ground by saguarro and saw the buckboard moving too fast and without rein, too far away for him to hear sounds, too distant to recognise the driver. He watched until he was sure there was trouble.

The vehicle bucked and bounced, wheels clear of the ground, heeled to the side and swirled away in dust. For a minute it was out of sight then reappeared. The wind veered and he heard the beat of hooves and the rattle of wheels and something else as well, a cry. At least he thought what he heard was a cry. He spurred the gelding and hurried.

The horse reached forward under him, neck stretching and mane flying, breasting a rise and following the slope of another in one long unbroken movement, throwing a trail of dust across the plain and sweeping round in a wide circle to come up behind the runaway.

Ahead of him the buckboard leaped, swerved and yawed behind two crazed horses. Wheels spun when they left the ground and rims shone bright. The gelding clawed at distance in grasping strides. Dust from the buckboard swirled back about his face. Ahead was the river. In the water the wagon would overturn and the horses fall, breaking tangled, splaying legs or necks and kicking each other to death in churned-up foam that would turn red.

Hoofbeats and wind raced past his ears. The buckboard writhed like a snake. He heard the cry again. He edged the gelding closer in flying dust till he was abreast and the three horses pounding the earth as one team. He did not look back.

When his knee touched the trace leather of the nearside team horse he eased boots from stirrups, reached out, filled his chest, threw his body forward in a grasping leap and held on. The gelding swung away and he was astride a sweating team animal, blinded by dust, deafened by wheel grind and the stamp of hoof. With-tight, he clutched at crest and leaned forward, grabbed a trailing rein, wound leather about wrist, straightened and hauled back. Horse sweat slung to his chin. The team veered as the river rushed into sight. The buckboard swung in a tight circle and slowed. He kept the rein short till fear and fight left the two panting horses and they halted, muzzles slavering. He hung on and sucked in air and the sound he heard then wasn't a cry but a long trembling moan, the sound of a human being falling headlong into the deep chasm of relief. The horses pulsed, shoulders quivering, nostrils hissing. Latigo looked over his shoulder and saw the woman begin to faint. He leaped and it was when he caught her up in his arms that he recognised the daughter of Matthew Kincaid.

He stood holding her, sunlight and sweat on his face, chest heaving, wondering what to do. There was no other living thing in sight.

Loose fair hair fell away from her forehead. He moved so that light shone on her face, drained of colour now and all the better for that because the arrogance had gone. Her skin was pale and fine, cheeks round and smooth, lips full-shaped and at peace; a lovely woman, limp and unconscious in his arms. This wasn't what he had expected to happen.

He walked to the river and laid her gently on the grass. There was no sound but the hissing of the water. He soaked his bandana and pressed the wet cloth to her temple.

The chill of the water made her move. He wet her lips and colour crept into her cheeks. Her breasts rose as she breathed again. She opened her eyes and saw his face close to her, sunburned forehead and high cheek-bones. He rose and stood away, tall, filling the sky, his voice coming from a distance.

"Rest easy," he said.

Buck Hemingway searched for Rebecca Nevin on the street and found her coming from behind the church. He stepped down from the roan and waited, the bundle in his arms. She was surprised, pleasure and welcome in her eyes, but for him talking wasn't easy. "Howdy, ma'am," he said. He glanced across his shoulder. "Your Pa's not around, is he?"

"No," she said. This was untrue. The sturdily built man with square face and dark moustache had come to the door of the livery stable and stood watching.

Someone else also saw what was happening. Joe Erskine, behind a window of the saloon, watched Buck get off his horse and wait for the girl to come near.

"What's that?" she asked.

He couldn't unroll the hide for her to see and it was too heavy and too big for her to carry. "It's kind of a present," he said. She did not respond. "It's for you."

"What is it, Buck?"

He shrugged gallantly. "Nothing much. Maybe you won't even like it."

"But I will, Buck. I'm sure I will. What is it?"

"It's a buffalo hide. You put it on the floor. It makes a rug."

"Where'd you get it?"

"Some Apaches came . . ."

"Indians!" she exclaimed.

"They were peaceable," he said quickly. "Came to our place two or three days ago."

"Didn't they try to kill you?"

"No, ma'am. They came in peace. They brought this buffalo skin for a present. Was really for Latigo, that's Mister Lansen, but he said I could have it."

"Weren't you afraid, Buck?"

63

"No, ma'am. I had a gun. Could have shot all three of them. There's a peace being made so we won't have any more Indian trouble. You want it?"

"Of course I want it. It's a lovely gift. Thank you very much. But I couldn't carry it, Buck. It's too heavy, isn't it?"

"Guess I should have thought of that."

"Couldn't you leave it at the livery stable? Papa will bring it home."

That was a dangerous thought. "Don't think I should meet your Pa right now," he hedged. "He might get mad at me, or something. Might think I was too forward . . . I mean bringing a present almost the first time I meet you."

"He won't mind."

"Thanks, ma'am, but I reckon not. Would it be all right if I left it with Ed Harrison? He's my friend. You could send somebody to pick it up."

"Are you afraid of my father, Buck?"

"Don't know, ma'am. I never met him. Reckon I am."

In the saloon Joe Erskine put the whisky to his lips and swallowed, not taking his eyes from the two over by the church. Ben Nevin leaned a hand on a door upright and watched with a great deal of interest. The young fellow's face wasn't familiar enough to recognise, and he wore a gun, but Rebecca didn't seem to mind so he supposed it was all right. He'd have to find out about him, though.

"You're very honest, Buck," she said. "But Papa won't shoot you."

"Thanks, ma'am. I'd rather not. Least, not yet."

"All right," she said. "You can leave it at the store. Papa will collect it. Thank you very much. I'm very flattered."

Buck glowed. "Reckon I'm flattered, too, ma'am," he said.

She ended it gently. "Good day, Buck. I hope I see you again."

"Yes, ma'am. You sure enough will."

He looked after her until she entered the church and closed the door. Joe Erskine watched him ride by the saloon, paid for the whisky and left. From the telegraph office where there was still no message, Buck rode to Harrison's. Ben Nevin also watched the yellow-haired youth ride along the sunlit street and wondered who he was, but when Buck dismounted at the store the livery stable owner knew where to enquire.

"What's that you're carrying, son?" Harrison asked at once.

"Buffalo hide, Mister Harrison."

"Could get you money for that. You aiming to sell it?"

"No, sir. Just leaving it here. It's . . . it's a present for Miss Rebecca Nevin. Her pa will collect it."

"She say she'd accept it, Buck?"

"Said she was flattered."

Harrison shrugged dolefully. "Guess you're hooked, then, boy. Hooked good."

"Huh?"

"Well, you know, don't you," explained the burly store-keeper. "Fellow gives a girl a present like that, he might just as well get right down on his bended knee and ask her proper. Same thing as getting your feet under the table. Else if he don't, her pa comes after him with a scatter gun."

"It's nothing like that, Mister Harrison! An Indian brought this here to Latigo and he passed it on to me. It's nothing more than a present."

"Presents are dangerous. She call you by your name yet, boy?"

"Yes, sir. She just did."

"Reckon you're doing well, Buck. What else can I do for you?"

"Latigo said I was to bring back some window glass."

"Sure . . ."

Buck left the store and was half-way along the street, glass in hand under arm, when Ben Nevin stepped on to the boardwalk at the store. The stable owner watched until Buck turned the corner and rode out of sight.

Nevin entered the store and stood before Ed Harrison. "Who is he, Ed?"

The question was like testing a silver dollar to see if it rang true. Harrison expected it the minute Nevin came through the door. He had no doubts at all about Buck Hemingway. "Name's Buck Hemingway. He's working for Latigo Lansen."

Nevin was sharply interested. "You mean there's a Lansen living?"

"Sure do. Rode in here a week or ten days ago, cool as

65

you please. Went first to the land office then came straight to me."

"What's he like?"

"Tall young fellow. Don't remember what he looked like before he left home but he's a fine looking man now."

"He aiming to stay?"

"That's what he says. He's got cattle coming from up north."

"What about Kincaid?"

Harrison shrugged. "It's Lansen land, Ben," he said. "He's got a right to stay on it. Taxes are paid. Fact is, he aims to stay on it, Kincaid or not. Just bought himself a gun."

"What about young Hemingway? He just talked to my girl Rebecca. I want to know about him."

"Son of Andrew Hemingway. Pulled out about two weeks ago."

"You mean he was driven out."

"That's what I mean. They were fine people."

"And the boy came back?"

"Don't know why, but he did. He's working for Latigo."

"Thanks, Ed. Just didn't want anybody from Kincaid's having anything to do with Rebecca."

"You don't need to do any worrying. The boy is respectable and he's got manners. That there bundle is something he brought in as a present for your girl. It's a buffalo hide. Said you'd pick it up."

"Buffalo hide, eh? Why didn't he leave it with me?"

"He's eighteen years old, Ben. Reckon he's a mite scared of meeting you."

Nevin laughed and lifted the bison skin. "Eighteen you say?"

Harrison nodded. "Why don't you ride out that way and talk to Latigo. You'll find him sociable."

"Thanks, Ed. I might just do that."

Some of the glass got broken and a sliding edge cut Buck's fingers when his roan started up at the sound of the shot. He tightened the rein. Joe Erskine rode out from behind a boulder with a gun in his hand. Buck stared and remembered, not afraid but wishing he didn't have to hold on to panes of window glass.

Erskine rode easy and loose in the saddle, lean body

66

swaying. He walked the horse closer, lips grinning. Buck Hemingway's face was straight and serious, his eyes clear; Erskine's were dark and amused. It had become funny when he realised that the man on the horse was only a boy. Light glinted on his dark skin. "Who are you, kid?" he asked.

Only Buck's lips moved. "What's it to you?"

The grin left Erskine's face. "Look, son, if you don't want a hole in the head, answer the question."

"Hemingway. Buck Hemingway."

Erskine's lips puckered. He regarded Buck from under lowered eyebrows. "Just saw you in town," he said. "You were talking to somebody."

"Is it against the law?"

Erskine straightened. "Now, look, boy, don't get uppity or I'll cut you down, sure's you're riding a horse! I aim to give you some advice. What's more, I aim for you to take it."

"Don't need advice, thanks."

Erskine raised the gun, pointed it and squeezed the trigger. The report was loud and both horses started up. Buck Hemingway's hat flew into the air. His belly tightened.

"You need this advice, boy," said Erskine. Buck's hand sweated on the panes of glass. "I see you talking to that girl again, I'll kill you."

"I'll talk to whoever I like!"

Erskine shrugged. "Fair enough, boy. You talk to her again and your folks'll have a burying party on their hands. What'd you say your name was?"

"Hemingway! But don't get the idea you frighten me."

Erskine remembered, strove to bring it closer. His face creased. He regarded Buck curiously. "Haven't I seen you somewhere?"

"You'll see me again, too!"

"Aren't you from that family we ran off? You Hemingway's son, from north of here?"

"That's right."

"You got your barn burned down, your water poisoned and your stock drove off." Erskine grinned and Buck wanted to kill him. "What're you doing here?"

"I came back!" Buck said.

Erskine laughed. "You didn't come back to fight us,

did you, boy? You don't aim to fight the Kincaid crowd all by yourself, do you?"

"Maybe."

Erskine raised the gun. Buck thought he was about to be killed. His body stiffened. The sneer left Erskine's face. "Look, kid, if I see you around that girl again I'll kill you, and I mean that for true! Now get out of here! Beat it!"

Buck tugged on the rein. The roan came round. He moved off toward the river. He rode for a mile, back-tracked and picked up his hat. There was a bullet hole in the side. He'd have to tell Latigo how he came to break some of the glass. And he sure as hell hated Joe Erskine.

Latigo Lansen had walked to a team horse to lay a hand on and calm a quivering flank. Now he came back. Hildy Kincaid looked up at him, not rising because if she did he might leave. She had recovered, her breasts at ease and colour deepening on her face. She wanted to talk and did not know how to begin. She did not hate him. It seemed necessary to talk to him.

"Thank you for what you did," she said. His shoulders moved. Anybody would have done the same thing. There was no need of thanks. He hung thumbs in his gunbelt. "Why don't you help me?" she said. He reached down a hand to assist her to rise but she made no move to accept the offer. "I don't mean to get up," she said.

"What kind of help, ma'am?"

"You could say something," she suggested.

His hands went back to the gunbelt. He looked about, scanning the plain, sunlight in his eyes, and came back to the river. Bell-like sounds hung in the air above the water.

"All this land," he said. She looked where he did and saw the same sights. Her thoughts were different. "Who owns it?" he asked.

"Some of it is ours. Some of it is yours."

He nodded. "That's a good thing to talk about."

"I never thought about it."

"There's a river between us," he said.

"That's split down the middle."

"What's needed here is a bridge."

She would have to make a choice, meet the offer he

68

made or turn away from it. "It shouldn't be hard to build," she accepted, not surprised at herself.

He met her eyes and nodded again. I guess it wouldn't, at that," he said. He looked away and again her eyes followed his. It was to the river and the yellow grass that he talked, not because he was afraid of anything that might appear on her face but because the land and the water were parts of what he had to say. "All that land, looking at it the way I do, is my future. I'm twenty-six years old, ma'am, and I've got time ahead of me. That's it ... all that grassland out there. That's the time I've got." There was light on his face. He did not look down at her. She watched and was silent, aware that here was a man talking about himself and about living and that what he said was important. "Land needs looking after and a man can't do it all by himself. He needs a woman to help him. I came back here because this is my home. I came to work the land and find a woman. That's what I aim to do."

It was calm and clear and easy to understand. "Are you not afraid?" she asked.

This time he did not avoid her eyes. "No, ma'am. A fellow gets scared of little things."

She stood up then. He was a bigger man than she had thought. Horses nibbled at grass. She walked to the buckboard. "They'll try to take it away from you," she said.

He recognised the first log of wood in the bridge. "I've ridden a horse half across this country, ma'am. Sometimes without a saddle. I can hold on good."

"You'll need to," she said. "They're determined men. And you're alone. Did anybody ever call you a brave man?"

"No, ma'am. Soldiered some but I got no medals."

"That's not the kind of bravery I mean," she said. At the buckboard she turned, another question in her mind. He did not look away. "What kind of woman do you hope to find? I mean to help you when you know there'll be trouble and danger."

"That's easy," he said. "The kind of woman who takes a fancy to a fellow and stays with him."

"Is she in Gila Bend?"

Another pine log. Soon there'd be a bridge with horses on it. "Yes, ma'am. She's in Gila Bend. Trouble is she doesn't know I am."

69

"Why don't you tell her?"

"Do that when I'm ready. Might have to break her down a piece."

He was talking about her. She stepped up on to the seat. He gathered the reins together and put them in her hands. "One thing about you, Mister Lansen," she said. "You wear pants."

"Figure a man ought to, ma'am. It's the natural thing."

She wheeled the team and the buckboard turned in a tight circle. There was more thinking to be done, about a bridge across the Gila river, or between two people. "Thanks for pulling up my team," she said.

He tipped his hat. "Was no trouble, ma'am."

She drove off and he watched her go. When the buckboard was out of sight he walked to the river and scooped water into his palm to drink. He sat on his haunches for minutes thinking about her.

CHAPTER SIX

BUCK came with a rush, yellow hair flying, standing stiff-legged in the stirrups and waving his hat. "Latigo!" he yelled and slid bonelessly from the saddle. Latigo walked out of the house. "Paydirt, Latigo!" Buck shouted. "Got a real nice message for you!"

Latigo hurried. "What's it say?"

"The stock's all bought and ready to move south. Here ... it's all wrote down. They're waiting for you to give the word!"

Buck had read the message a dozen times and read it again across the arm and hand that shook as Latigo scanned the words on the paper. He read the message and gazed past the Indian lance in its circle of white stones. "They'll come in from the north, Buck," he said.

"Sure! Won't touch the town that way. I'll bet you're glad, Latigo!"

Latigo's eyes went back to the slip of paper. The fever that had made Buck ride like a wanted man began in his own veins. "Two thousand head!" he said. "We're taking hold, Buck! We're taking hold!"

"Can hear them bellowing already, Latigo! Sure's a gun I can. They're out there now yelling for water!"

Latigo laughed out loud. Buck's eyes shone. "This is the best day yet, Latigo. Huh?"

Latigo clenched his hands. He stared into Buck's corn-coloured eyes. The intensity was dangerous and catching. What happened then was between two grown men gripped by sudden, disrobing, human joy. Latigo drove a balled-up fist hard against Buck's square shoulder. His lips uttered the sound he should have made the minute he saw the ranch-house for the first time after ten years. He yelled out loudly and wordlessly. Buck's eyes widened as Latigo crushed the telegraph paper into a ball, whipped it in the air and yelled. Buck echoed with a high clear "Yippeee!", mouth wide, chest and belly flattened to make it loud and long. When Latigo swung an arm and swiped the hat from Buck's head in a high flying arc out over the pump and water butt, the yellow-headed youth shouted in protest and delight. "Hey! My hat!"

They stared at each other, bodies tight, waiting. There had to be something more because crying out wasn't enough. Straining lungs didn't do all that had to be done or waste the energy that had to be expended. Latigo threw himself forward and butted Buck on the chest. The boy fell away sprawling, legs and arms flailing, mouth open and yelling, eyes dancing. He slid a full yard on the ground and lay on his back staring at the sun, speechless. Latigo leaped. Buck shouted defensively. Together they wrestled in dust and sunlight.

Latigo sprang away and stood with body held forward, knees bent and hand close to the gun. The game was violent, the reason strident. Latigo carried it further. "All right!" he shouted. "I'm the sheriff and you're a crazy gunslinger! Reach for your iron, mister!"

Buck scrabbled on the ground, the mood like wine, dragged feet under him, rose to one knee and stretched out a hand. "I'm warning you, sheriff," he said earnestly. "I don't want to kill you but when I get up off this ground I'll have a gun in my hand!"

"Try me, mister!" shouted Latigo. "I've killed men like you before. Get on your feet, gunslinger! Come up shooting!"

Buck steadied himself, drew a foot in under and rested

71

on haunches. His eyes darted quickly, seeking escape. Latigo sneered. "Scared, gunslinger?" he snarled.

Buck's chest heaved, his breathing loud.

Latigo did what was necessary. Still hollow-bellied, he unbuckled the gunbelt and tossed it aside. Buck straightened and did likewise. They faced each other and again Buck reached out a hand. "I swear, Sheriff, I'm going to hurt you!" he announced. "I'm bigger than you. I'll bend you over till I hear your back snap clear in two!"

Buck rushed forward. Latigo stepped to the side. Buck came charging like a young bull, all shoulders and heft. They closed, grappling, on the ground, legs stretching and boots furrowing. Muscles strained till the end was pain, chests heaved and shoulders thrust. They wrestled and it was Latigo who turned out to be the stronger. Buck yelled out hoarsely in surrender and when Latigo stood away breathless, lay on the ground on his back, exhausted, lungs bursting, arms and legs sore.

Latigo walked to the water butt and doused his head, the passion spent. He rested on the lip of the trough and palmed his face. "We're crazy, Buck," he said.

Buck crawled on the ground and rose slowly. "We're crazy all right," he agreed and gulped air. "You know something, Latigo? Until this minute I was the strongest man I knew."

"You're eighteen years old and we're crazy," said Latigo. "Because we've got two thousand head of cattle coming south, we beat hell out of each other."

Buck's face widened. "You didn't hurt me, mister! But you sure know how to wrestle a man. I guess it's because we're glad, the cattle coming and all. Anyway, it was good. Fellow's got to let off steam some time."

Latigo regarded the powerful youth before him. It might have been something else as well, something Buck didn't know about; a river and a bridge of pine logs thrown across, or a woman waiting for you to get down from your horse.

Buck walked to where his gunbelt lay in the dust.

"You answer the message, Buck?" asked Latigo. "Did you give them the word to start moving?"

Buck straightened and turned. "No, sir. I didn't give them any word."

72

"You should have," said Latigo. "You've got an interest in those cattle now."

"All I own is what I'm standing in, Latigo."

Latigo disagreed. "Some of the cattle you own, too," he said. Buck stared. "Ride back into town and send the message. Give them the word to start the herd south." Buck strode to the horse. Latigo turned at the sound of hoofbeats and raised a hand. "Wait, Buck . . ."

A single rider came in sight, walked the horse on the draw and reined. Matthew Kincaid saw Latigo Lansen standing by the water butt, gun and gunbelt on the ground at his feet; and Buck by the flank of his horse, hand on saddle horn ready to mount. Motion had ceased the moment he appeared. The rancher eased the sorrel nearer.

Latigo and Buck watched the rider approach. Kincaid looked from one to the other before he spoke. "You're not wearing guns, Lansen," he said. "How're you going to kill me if I get down?"

Latigo moved a hand towards Buck. "He has a gun."

"He hasn't got the same reason to kill me."

"He's got better reasons," said Latigo. "What can I do for you?"

The man on the sorrel looked at Buck. "Don't intend to get off my horse so you won't need the gun, Lansen," he said. "What I have to say is private."

"There's nothing Buck can't listen to."

"He can't listen to what I've got to say."

Buck moved. "Got to go into town, anyway," he said. Latigo nodded permission. Buck climbed into the saddle and turned the horse. "I'll do what you said, Latigo."

"Take care of yourself."

"Yes, sir."

Kincaid looked over his shoulder and watched till Buck was out of sight. The rancher had two reasons for coming and one of them could be stated immediately. He relaxed in the saddle, hands clasped about the horn. "Rode over to say thanks for what you did for my daughter day before yesterday."

"She was in trouble," Latigo said. "Any man would have helped the lady."

"You were there. You're the one I've got to thank."

"Think nothing of it. Was glad to help."

73

Kincaid moved in the saddle. "You and I are kind of enemies, Lansen," he said.

"That doesn't mean I'm your daughter's enemy."

Kincaid regarded him carefully, thought about the statement made, and nodded. What Latigo had said was connected with the rancher's second reason for coming. "You've got some nice land here, Lansen," he said. "Plenty of work for a man."

"I've got help."

"Yes, the boy," said Kincaid and paused. "Help can be hired if help's all you want." He paused again and looked about. His eyes fastened on the ranch-house. "A man gets lonely on his own," he said. "I know. Been a lonely man for a long time."

"People live with it."

"I know, but you're a young man. It's harder for you. Ought to get yourself a wife, Lansen."

Hairs on the back of Latigo's neck pricked. He wasn't sure, didn't know what to think, was afraid to in case he was right and had to turn angry and hot. "What's that supposed to mean?"

The man on the horse straightened. He did not look away from Latigo Lansen's upturned face. "I've got a fine looking daughter, Lansen," he said bluntly. "She needs a husband. You need a wife. How do you feel about that?"

"You tell her you were coming here?"

"Didn't see any need to tell her. Seems to me that it would be a sensible arrangement. You'd get yourself a nice looking, capable woman who wouldn't be a burden to you."

There was no anger; no need for rage. What the rancher said wasn't worth honest heat. "That's the lowest thing I ever heard, Kincaid," said Latigo. "You're willing to sell your daughter to get my land."

"Nobody said anything about land."

"It didn't have to be said. That's why you're here. If you were a snake I'd shoot you and throw the carcase on the roof to rot!"

"You're talking out of turn, Lansen," Kincaid said. "I came here with a proposition. I came to talk as one man to another. What we discuss is private and my daughter doesn't have to be told. Living out here is rough and people do the best they can. Not so many women about that a man can be choosey, not so many upstanding

74

men about that a woman doesn't grab what's likely."

"Doesn't she have anything to say?"

"You didn't listen, Lansen," said Kincaid. "I said people out here match up quick because there's work to be done and there's no time. A man needs a woman and any woman is willing to be a wife."

Lines creased Latigo Lansen's forehead. His back straightened. "When I need a riding horse, Kincaid," he said. "I ride out and throw my rope around the best broomtail I see. Then I bring him in and I break him. After that he's mine. I find him and I break him and I own him. I'll do the same with my woman. I don't need any help!"

Kincaid stared down. "The trouble with you, Lansen, is that you're mule-headed. But mules can be made to work. I'm a bigger man than you. I'm rich. I own a lot of land around here. I'll drive you out, Lansen, then you'll have nothing. I'm offering you a chance to stay and a chance to live that you won't get a second time!"

Latigo reached for his gunbelt and drew out the Colt. "Get off my land!" he ordered. "I own it. I'm staying on it. Don't come back here unless you want to sell your range!"

Kincaid's face paled. His hands tightened on the saddle horn. "I'll hurt you, Lansen," he threatened. "I swear it. You'll come crawling to me before I'm finished!"

"Snakes crawl, Kincaid. I'm a grown man. Get off my land!"

Kincaid wheeled the sorrel and did not look back. Latigo buckled the gunbelt about his waist and leaned hands on the rim of the water trough. The water reflected the sky and the drift of cloud that fanned from the west. Minutes ago he had been yelling with the pain of gladness. Minutes ago he was so sure of himself that he was glad to be living and upright. Minutes ago.

He straightened to find a man on a horse in front of him, a broad-faced man with a moustache who dismounted and held out his hand.

" 'Day, Mister Lansen. Least I reckon you're Mister Lansen."

"I'm Lansen."

The grip was strong and honest. "The name's Nevin."

Latigo remembered. "We met before," he said.

"We didn't talk that day," said Nevin. "I was busy.

Guess I was too angry to talk. You just watched."

"Was none of my business."

"You did the right thing," Nevin assured. "I do my own fighting." He rested hands on his belt and came to the purpose of his visit. "Didn't ride all the way out here to take up your time. Came to ask you a straight question about the young fellow you have working for you."

"He doesn't need a job," Latigo said quickly. "He's staying with me."

"Didn't intend to take the boy away from you, Mister Lansen. All I wanted was for you to settle my mind."

"What about?"

Nevin fingered his chin, looked up quickly. "You're not old enough to have my problem," he said. "But this young fellow of yours . . . well, he's kind of took up with my daughter . . ."

"Buck is only eighteen years old, Mister Nevin."

"The name's Ben," said Nevin. "We're not fighting each other so I don't reckon we have to be formal."

Latigo accepted the second handshake. "Thanks," he said. "My given name's Latimer. People call me Latigo."

"Glad to," said Nevin. "I don't aim to interfere in my daughter's life, Latigo, except to protect her. That's why I was chastising Joe Erskine."

"You don't need to worry about Buck," said Latigo. "He's a good man. I'm proud to know him. Going to make him my partner."

Nevin nodded. "Thanks," he said. "That's what I came for. You've eased my mind. The boy is welcome at my house any time. You tell him that." He climbed back into the saddle and fixed his hat. He looked down. "You know, Latigo, you've taken on quite a job here. I mean aiming to stay with all the trouble you'll have."

"The trouble's started already."

"Reckon it has. Saw Kincaid riding away as I came up. That kind of trouble is always in a hurry." Nevin leaned on the saddle horn. "A man's not always alone, Latigo," he said. "Sometimes he's got friends he doesn't even know about."

"How does he get to find them?"

Nevin laughed and straightened. "Why, if he's got a voice in his throat at all, he yells out loud and clear and they come running."

76

"Thanks, Ben Nevin," said Latigo. "When it gets serious, you'll hear me."

"I'll be listening."

It became serious that night. What he expected came with the suddenness of a pistol shot. The thing he had waited for, had gone riding out over the range looking for, came right up to his door and it hurt, as Kincaid said it would.

It was dark, the sky clouded, with only glimmers of light shining through. And there was no wind, which turned out to be a good thing.

Buck rode home at sundown, hurrying by the side of the river that was all aglow, sheeted with copper light. The sky burned in hot distance and dark shadows lay on the ground. Face bronze and hands ebony he carried a sack with care. He slid from the saddle and was curious about Kincaid. "What happened, Latigo? I'd sure like to know."

Latigo stripped down the horse. "Not a thing, Buck," he lied. "I picked up my gun."

"You mean he just went? He didn't do anything?"

"That's right."

"Why'd he come then . . . if he just turned around and went back?"

"Don't know, Buck. He didn't say. What've you got in the sack?"

Buck untied the cord and reached in a hand. Latigo heard the flutter of wings. "Got us a broody hen and fourteen eggs," Buck announced. "Going to put her down in the barn."

Latigo eyed him. "Chickens don't lay eggs for a long time, Buck," he said. "You aim to stay in these parts?"

"Yes, sir. I sure do!"

Latigo headed for the house. "Come inside and I'll tell you what Ben Nevin said."

Buck's eyes widened. "Was he here?" He followed Latigo part of the way, sack in one hand, broody hen in the other. "He wasn't looking for me, was he, Latigo? Did he have a gun?"

"Come in the house."

"Can't do that till I put the hen on the eggs. What'd he want, Latigo? What'd he say?"

77

Latigo turned at the door. "Wanted to know if you were a fit man to be seeing Rebecca."

"What'd you say, Latigo? What'd you say?"

"Tell you when you come in."

"Latigo!"

It was dark when it happened, the sky deep, stars hidden, windbreak silent and the river only a hiss of sound. It began with the stamp of hooves and the crash of breaking glass.

Buck shot upright in bed, staring into darkness. Latigo stiffened. Bullets spattered on stone walls. Glass scattered in slivers. "Latigo!"

Latigo sprang from the bed. "Get your clothes on!" he shouted. "And stay down!"

Buck moved. "What're they doing, Latigo? What do they want?" Windows exploded into tiny unseen diamonds. "All that glass I put in!" he shouted.

"Buck! Keep down!" ordered Latigo.

Night clothed the men outside. They remained hidden. Latigo's hand groped in darkness for the Winchester. High-pitched rifle bullets pierced the outside blackness. Buck crept close to a window.

"Buck!" shouted Latigo. "Get back!"

"Get back where? They're out front!"

"Go in the bedroom and stay down low!"

"I can't see from there!"

"This is not your fight. Do what I tell you!"

Buck leaned hands on the wooden floor. "Let me stay, Latigo."

He did not have time to answer and refuse. The night crackled with gunfire. Bullets spat on walls and door and windows and chimney square. Glass fell in splinters on the beds and told the men inside that the house was surrounded. Horses snorted. He crept to a window and raised the rifle, waiting. "Did they do this to you, Buck?"

The answer came out of darkness. "Yes, sir. We fought them off a couple of times. Ma used a gun, too. But they got at us by houghing our cattle. That's what hurt most ... having to go out next day and kill the stock that had been hamstrung."

"This is the second time," Latigo said. "This time I've got to kill somebody."

78

"Reckon it's too dark to do that. They picked a good night."

The shooting stopped. Silence rushed in. Latigo waited, ready, rifle barrel on the window ledge. He heard Buck breathing. In the outer darkness a horse moved and a voice called out. Latigo's hand tightened on gunstock.

"Lansen!" cried the voice.

He didn't answer.

"Lansen! If you can hear me, call out! Loud and now!"

He leaned his face close to the empty window frame. "Get off my land, Kincaid!" he shouted.

The darkness broke open. Guns crackled, window curtains leaped inwards, ripped by lead. Latigo raised the rifle and returned the fire. Buck flung himself to a window and pushed a Colt six-gun through broken glass. He fired out into the dark without seeing a target. Chips of stone sparked away from outside walls. Bullets flattened in a leaden smallpox. More glass fell. Latigo searched the blackness for the figure of a man on a horse but the night lay like a blanket, impenetrable.

There was silence again. Buck's loud breathing filled the room. Latigo held out a hand for quiet and forgot that he could not be seen. "Quiet, Buck!"

The voice called out again, strident and loud.

"Lansen! You've got the boy in there. We don't aim to hurt him. If you hear me, come out! You hear?"

"I hear you!"

Buck crouched on the floor, close to Latigo. "Latigo, don't! They'll shoot you down for sure!"

"I'm staying, Buck!"

The voice again.

"Come out, Lansen! Else we'll come in and get you!"

Latigo squeezed the trigger of the Winchester. A bullet sang its way towards the voice. "Come on!" he yelled.

Horses began to move with a wild stampede of hooves. Noise encircled the house. "Keep down, Buck!" shouted Latigo.

The raiders swept in close, guns firing, ten or twelve in a bunch, rushing close to door and windows. They wheeled and broke, a river of men on horses spreading into darkness. Latigo emptied the rifle, sprang and ran to the bedroom. He used the Colt as a wave of sound from hooves surged behind the house. Buck flung himself from window to window, firing blindly until the hammer of the pistol snapped on empty chambers. He crouched in a corner to reload. Latigo knelt and thumbed bullets into the Winchester. The men outside retreated in a clatter of hoofbeats.

"They'll come again," Buck said. His forehead sweated and he didn't know.

The horsemen came racing back, beating the ground, rushing out of the dark, blacker than the night and still not seen; sound shapes that swept forward like flapping shrouds. The night became ugly with the noise of hooves and guns and voices, bit and bridle, yell and shout and the snort of nostril. Spits of white flame cut into shadow and left wounds of powder smoke.

Latigo and Buck waited for it to come again. Their bodies were held tight, their eyes narrowed. When the raiders were close Winchester rifle and Colt pistol sent spears of light into darkness. Horses reared up and splayed away, forelegs fighting. The air thickened with the smell of burned powder. The night swelled with the noise of stamping animals and the voices of horsemen who clung to arched backs and rising saddles. Bullets beat upon outside walls and ended.

Buck sucked air into his lungs. He reached for shells and spun the chamber of the Colt. Latigo knelt on the floor and fingered bullets into the rifle. The flood of sound outside drained away. Buck peered over the window ledge. "Can't see a thing, Latigo," he breathed. "Too dark. They sure picked their night to come." He pressed shoulder-blades against cold stone and breathed. Latigo listened and said nothing. For a minute there was silence. Hooves beat the ground again.

"Here they come!"

Buck knelt, gun ready on the window lip, teeth hard together. The riders stormed about the house. A horse pranced and reared, forelegs in the air beating down the sound of guns and its own fear, close enough for the fawn, sweat-streaked belly to be seen. Buck raised the gun and fired, finger tight about the trigger, palm fanning the hammer. Six shots ripped from the barrel of the Colt. The horse whinnied and threshed and the man on its

80

back yelled out and crashed to the ground with a cry of death on his lips.

"Got one, Latigo!" Buck shouted. "Got one!"

The wave of sound backed towards the river. A riderless horse shrilled in the air and galloped into the night. Latigo reloaded quickly. Buck's hands shook as he filled the Colt. "We can hold them off, Latigo, can't we?"

Latigo jacked the lever of the rifle. "They're not coming in here, Buck," he said.

Buck stood with his back to the wall, body straight and tight, the gun at arms length by his side. He trembled. He palmed sweat from his face and lips and was unable to satisfy his need for air. "Latigo," he said through the darkness. "Latigo . . . I never killed a man before."

Latigo heard the tremor on the boy's lips. It wasn't fear. "They're trying to kill you," he said. "You did right."

The voice called again. Latigo held up a hand for silence. Buck did not see and was quiet, anyway. "Lansen! This is your last chance! You coming out?"

Latigo raised himself, pointed the rifle in the direction of the voice and squeezed the trigger. "Come and get me!" he yelled. Fear clutched at his belly and for the moment that it took the words to leave his lips wondered if he had done right. He was afraid for Buck, standing somewhere near in the darkness, numbed by the knowledge that he had killed a man. The boy was eighteen years old, fighting a battle that wasn't his; he had a gun in his hand and he was killing men who were not his enemies.

Latigo shouldn't have said that.

"Buck!"

"Latigo?"

"Go in the back room!"

"What for?"

"Go in the back room. Lie down on the floor close to the wall and stay there."

"I'm staying here, Latigo!"

"Buck! Do what I tell you!"

"Latigo! I just killed a man! I'm not running away. I'm not hiding. I'm staying right here!"

There wasn't time to insist. The horses started moving. This time the darkness was gashed by flaming brushwood. The raiders rushed forward, far apart, burning torches held high. A fusillade of bullets spattered like hail against the house. Glass fell inwards.

"Trying to burn us out!" yelled Buck. "Latigo!"

Men on horses rode close. Smoking brands lit the darkness as they whooshed through air to the roof. Dry shingles crackled. The night became red, streaked with yellow tongues. A tied bundle of burning twigs crashed on a glassless window and broke apart. Bullet-riddled curtains smoked and burst into flame. The room filled with smoke and dancing light.

Latigo wrenched at burning window shades and stamped the cloth to smouldering rags. Buck kicked blazing brushwood into corners and beat at licking flames with his bare hands. Bullets whanged on stone. Wooden splinters shot away from the inside of the pine-log door. Outside, the crackle of rising flame rose above the stamp of hooves and the shouts of horsemen. Latigo flung himself to a window and fired at rushing figures. A pawing horse reared up in reddened dark and a blazing brand raced to the window with a hissing whap. Burning wood thrust at his chest. Buck slashed at remaining window glass and fired blindly into smoke and flame-invested darkness. Gushes of fire fell from the roof. Cascades of sparks spouted down and scorching, acrid smoke coiled from the bedroom. Latigo rolled on the floor, tore the burning shirt from his back and ran to the window, rifle to sweat-streaked shoulder.

Flames spiralled from the shingled roof. The night became bright with long red sheets of fire. A spark-laden smoke column reached upwards to the sky. Buck held hands to his belly and bent low, choking on resined air. Latigo shouted.

"Buck! Get out of here!"

The boy's voice rasped in his throat. "I'll go when you do."

"Damn you, Buck!"

"Sure, Latigo."

Burning rafters fell from the roof. Sparks exploded in the air and poured down, like worms of light. Flaming joist wood hit Latigo's naked shoulders. He fell and yelled and fought clear.

"Come out, Lansen!" commanded the voice. "Come out or burn!"

Red darkness clothed horses and men and made them hellish phantoms. Flames fled into the sky. Flickering shadows snaked on the ground. Latigo damned the men outside.

He hauled Buck from the corner by the shoulders, the boy's face blackened, his lungs rasping. He shouted and forced the youth upright. "We're getting out, Buck!" he yelled. "Stand up, damn you, stand up!" He dragged the boy to the door. Buck leaned shoulders on wall stones. Latigo slid back the wooden bolt. "When I open this door they'll start shooting!" he shouted. "Wait till it stops, then run! Get on the ground and make for cover. You hear me, Buck? You listening?"

"You go first, Latigo!"

"Do as I tell you!" ordered Latigo.

Behind them the roof began to fall inwards. Flaming rafters pointed down, exploding in smoke and hissing fire, hung suspended for moments, ripped loose and fell crazily. Latigo choked, flung open the plank door and clung to the wall. Smoke and flame spouted out. The sound of guns rose above the hiss and crackle of fire. Bullets rushed at the door and beat on stone, then ceased.

He grabbed at Buck. "Now!" he shouted.

Together they rushed out into fire-haunted darkness, eyes swimming. The burning ranch-house spewed and gushed upwards. Buck twisted and hit the ground, the wind knocked out of him. He crawled on earth, crouched and rose and ran. Men on horses shouted. Guns exploded. Latigo pointed his Colt and fired.

"Ride them down!" yelled the voice.

Horses came thundering out of a furnace of black and yellow smoke. Buck saw too late. He yelled as fire-brightened forelegs threshed the air above him. He held hands and arms about his head and face. Hooves filled the air, hooves and smoke and red streaks of light. He went down under it all.

"Buck!" yelled Latigo. His shout was drowned by hooves. He cursed shapeless figures shrouded by smoke. He sprawled on the ground. Earth scored his chest and shoulders. He haunched to the water trough and dragged himself close.

"Ride him down!" insisted the voice.

Latigo's belly tied itself into a knot. He sucked in air.

Buck lay on the ground somewhere, body trampled by hooves, face burned and blackened, maybe dead, and Latigo hated the men who had done it.

He raised hand and gun over the lip of the water tank. The movement was seen and men came riding with shouts and guns. His pistol shone red, hot to the touch; there was no air in his lungs and his heart beat like a whipped drum skin. He lay flat on his back, head touching the wood of the water trough, held the gun in both hands and fired the Colt straight up into the belly of the first horse that came leaping in a great noisy, flame-lit arc over his head. The animal shuddered and collapsed in mid-air, crashed in a wide leg and neck-breaking sprawl, whinnied shrilly and died. The rider rolled clear and ran. Yards away he sank to his knees and clasped arms about his middle.

There were others. They came in a bunch. He used the gun till the chamber was empty and three horses lay coughing blood.

Anger brought water to his eyes. The same anger forced sounds out of his mouth that he did not know about. When the pistol was empty he stood up, red and yellow flame-light on his naked chest and shoulders, and ran towards the men on horses. Behind him the house burned fiercely.

Smoke coiled in the air. A rider eased his horse forward. Latigo shouted sounds, not words and, because there were no more bullets, hurled the gun. The rider brought out his pistol and pointed it down. His eyes reflected the glow of the burning ranch-house. He squeezed the trigger and a great red blackness thrust against Latigo Lansen. The ground rushed up.

The rider looked back for instructions.

"Pick up our men," said the voice.

They did that and rode away. Hoofbeats faded into darkness.

The roof of the house caved inwards with a wild eruption of sparks. Flame and smoke spouted to the sky in a geyser of black and red and yellow. Window glass burst from frames that crackled as they burned. The pine-plank door hissed loudly. Unused bullets exploded. Water in the trough glistened red and reflected skyclimbing light.

After the fire came silence. The windbreak rustled. The river came into its own, running dark, rippling at the edges. Soon there was only smoke that thinned to thread-like wisps of vapour. Hour away, morning lighted the eastern sky. One by one the fallen horses sighed and died.

Before the sky cleared and the shadows that draped the wind-break melted down into strands of mist, Buck moved on the ground. He stared at the greying sky, thoughts coming from far off and not staying long with him. Ideas were hard to hold on to and he didn't know what he was thinking. He heard the ripple of the river and did not recognise the sound. His face burned and all of his body hurt. Twice he forced his shoulders off the earth and twice he hit the ground again with a gasp of air that hurt him inside. He rolled and pushed hands against the dirt. His head spun crazily and he wanted to cry out. He stared at the ground below him, willing it to stay in one place. When remembrance rushed back he rested on hands and knees.

"Latigo!" he called. "Latigo!"

He bent his head to water, filled his mouth and spewed, palmed his face and chin and gazed at the blackened ruin of the ranch-house. Wisps of blue curled slowly from charred timbers, stonework was smoked black, the door hung askew, pinewood burned to charcoal. He turned and walked toward the river. When he saw the bare-chested figure on the ground he ran forward and knelt.

"Latigo!"

His hand touched Latigo's shoulder. The flesh was warm. Buck turned him over. Blood streaked chest and arms but there was a heartbeat. He tugged the shirt from his back, ripped the chambray from seam to seam, ran to the river and soaked the cloth. When cold water touched his skin. Latigo moved his head.

Buck dabbed at the shoulder wound. "Latigo," he repeated. "Latigo . . . Wake up! It's me . . . It's Buck, Latigo. Wake up!"

Latigo moved, filled his lungs and groaned. Buck wet the shirtcloth again, bathed the face of the man on the ground and held his head. It was a long time before Latigo opened his eyes and saw the scorched forehead above him and Buck's eyes probing his own. Then he remembered. He nodded. Buck sighed mightily in relief. "Sure glad you're not dead, Latigo," he said. "Rest easy now. I'll ride into town and fetch the doctor."

But Latigo's hand gripped the boy's wrist and held on. He didn't speak and Buck didn't ride.

CHAPTER SEVEN

BUCK turned from cinching the gelding. He watched Latigo Lansen untie the knot with fingers and teeth and ease his arm from the bandana sling. He was afraid of what might happen. Four days ago he had probed a bullet out of Latigo's shoulder flesh. "You shouldn't ride, Latigo," he protested.

Smoke no longer rose from the burned-out ranch-house, the embers cold now. Latigo hadn't once looked at the house, had been silent most of the time.

"Got to ride, Buck. Something I have to do."

"No, you don't. You figure there's something to be done, I'll do it."

"Some things a man does for himself."

He took the reins in his good hand, pushed a boot into the stirrup and then stood down again. Buck waited. Latigo gazed past him to the blackened shell of the house, hard stone walls and gaping window spaces. "Buck," he said. "I want you to saddle your horse and ride back to your folks."

The boy knew it would be something like this, had felt it in his bones, had seen it in Latigo's silence and tightened lips. The disappointment in expectation had been as hard to bear as the reality now of hearing it said. "I'm not going," he decided simply and said so.

"You'll get hurt.'

"I've been hurt before."

"I want you to go."

Buck gripped his gunbelt. "Stop talking, Latigo," he said. "I'm staying. You've got cattle coming. You said some of them were mine."

"I'm going to fight back, Buck. People will be hurt."

"You'll need help."

"Not the way I intend to fight."

"You can't do it all yourself. I'm not going, Latigo. I'm a grown man and I've got a right to do what I want. I'm staying."

Latigo didn't argue any more. He stepped into the

86

saddle and wheeled the horse. He rode south for a mile, then crossed the river by the aspen where the river willow hung low and wrote its name on the water. The sun was high, the sky clear. When he eased the horse out of the water he was on Kincaid land. To the south of him grazed a thousand head of cattle, farther south another thousand. The main herd lay west. Inside a week Lansen cattle would suck at the same Gila river water.

He hated Kincaid for what he had done and he believed that he hated the woman.

When he came in sight of the house he reined. Smoke climbed from a chimney and there were horses in the corral. He heard sounds but saw no Kincaid riders.

He made his gun comfortable and straightened his back, walked the gelding between long-horn pillars and slowed when he reached the giant saguarro. The wide front door was open to the sunlight. Saddles lined the corral rail. A man's voice came from the bunkhouse and all that should be happening on a ranch this size was taking place. So he wasn't expected.

He stood down and strode to the verandah steps. A lace curtain fluttered behind an upstairs window and rapid steps sounded on the stairs. Hildy Kincaid walked out into the light. For moments neither she nor Latigo Lansen spoke.

He searched her face for the thoughts behind. He had talked about what was nearest to his mind and she knew what he meant. Some of the logs that would have joined two stretches of territory and two people together would have come from her side of the river.

She saw him straight but tired, eyes different and lips set in a tight line. And there seemed to be something unnatural about the way he carried his left arm, as though it hurt and needed protection. She was glad he had come and waited for a sign from him. Pride might account for the defiance in his eyes.

From where he stood she had changed. There was still the same flush of color on her cheeks, the same upright carriage, but softened now and gentler; lovely instead of proud. Her eyes were bright in hesitant welcome, her lips parted ready to talk to him. There didn't seem to be any reason for fighting, except that she still carried the riding whip.

The silence between them ended when she moved down the steps. He nodded and she noticed that he did not move his arm at all.

" 'Day, ma'am."

"Good day, Mister Lansen. Won't you come into the house?"

"No, ma'am. I'll do my talking here."

He had changed. His voice was different, harder and without any promise.

"Did you come to see my father?"

"Anybody called Kincaid will do."

She began to be afraid. Something had happened that she didn't know about. "My name is Kincaid," she said slowly.

He looked straight at her and she did not turn away. He saw the question in her eyes and ignored it. "Your father's a coward, ma'am," he said. She stiffened. Her hands clasped the stick of the crop and the colour of cactus blossom on her face deepened to scarlet. "First time I came here he sent his daughter out to talk for him . . ."

"That's not true, Mister Lansen. Father was resting . . ." she interrupted and halted when she remembered that her father hadn't been resting at all but standing at the back of the hall watching what went on.

"The second time I come he sends his daughter out to do his talking," said Latigo. "Seems to me the only time he's willing to talk is when he's on a horse or has a dozen hired guns behind him."

"You're wrong," she defended. "My father is not afraid of anything living."

"Neither am I, ma'am," he said. "Since you're here I'll tell you why I came."

"Don't," she said quickly. "I'll bring my father." Halfway to the verandah steps she halted and looked back. "Has something happened since I saw you?"

He was unable to read anything on her face. "Yes, ma'am. It's why I'm here."

"Would you like to tell me about it . . . whatever it was?"

"You said you'd get your father," he returned. "One telling will do."

"You think I know about it."

He didn't look away. "Your name's Kincaid."

"Yes," she said. "That's a kind of brand, isn't it?"

88

"It's a brand that doesn't carry much credit," he said.
Her eyes glistened. "You're trying to humiliate me,
Mister Lansen," she said.

"Yes, ma'am. That's the way it's got to be done."

"You could be wrong," she said. "You don't have to
beat me into submission. I wanted that bridge as much as
you." He did not answer. She turned from him and
mounted the steps. "I'll fetch father."

Matthew Kincaid walked out of the great polished door
and stood at the edge of the verandah. He did not show
any surprise that Latigo was not dead. His daughter followed and stood to the side, her eyes on Latigo.

"Aren't you scared I'll shoot you, Lansen?" asked
Kincaid. "You're on my land and you're not on your
horse."

"I'd kill you first, Kincaid," said Latigo. "I'm a better
shot and I'm quicker."

Kincaid squared his shoulders. "What do you want?"

Latigo rested a hand on his gun handle. Kincaid observed but his face did not change. The woman did not
look away from the man on the ground and it was about
the woman that his first question was concerned.

"Does your daughter know what happened five nights
ago, Kincaid?"

The rancher glanced sharply at his daughter. She
caught the swift regard. Her eyes clouded and stayed on
her father. Latigo noted the doubt and question on her
face.

"That's a crazy question, Lansen," said Kincaid. "What
did happen?"

Latigo's hand caressed the gun handle. It could be that
she did not know. Maybe it was true that she wanted the
bridge as much as himself. "My ranch-house was burned
down," he said calmly and watched her body become
rigid. "My partner was ridden down by mounted men, and
I was shot."

She responded immediately. "Father! What is this?"

Kincaid shrugged. "It's news to me," he said. "What
are you getting at, Lansen? A bunch of crazy Indians tear
up your place and you come yelping to me!"

"Not Indians," said Latigo. "Kincaid riders and Kincaid
himself."

The rancher's face reddened. "Are you calling me a liar?"

Latigo nodded his head. "I know your voice, Kincaid. Nobody else wants me dead."

She spoke quickly. "Father . . . " she began.

Kincaid bristled. "Go in the house, Hildy. I'll deal with this crazy man."

"You called out to me, Kincaid," reminded Latigo. "Come out or burn! Remember?"

"I don't know what you're talking about, Lansen!"

"Father! Tell me . . ."

"You know, Kincaid," said Latigo. "You were there."

"You were, father! You were out riding five nights ago. Every man on the ranch was with you."

"Stop talking, girl! Go in the house! What do you want, Lansen? Why did you come here?"

Latigo took his hand from the gun. It was the wrong thing to do but he did not know that Erskine was watching or that history would repeat itself so clearly. "To tell you one thing, Kincaid," he said. "The only way you'll get my land is to kill me. I came here to work and be a good neighbour but that's not the way you want things or the way you see the future. You'll be sorry you ever heard the name of Lansen. You never figured that anybody would fight back but that's what I intend to do. You won't like it and it will end in one way, Mister Kincaid. You'll be dead or I will."

Kincaid shouted angrily. "You're not big enough to threaten me, Lansen! I own this valley!"

Latigo didn't hear the footsteps in time. They came from behind. But the woman cried out and he turned too late. For the second time in weeks Joe Erskine hit him with the side of a gun.

Kincaid reached forward and stopped. Erskine stepped back, lips and eyes pleased. The woman raced down the steps, raised the whip and slashed angrily at Erskine's dark-skinned face. Her father's forehead creased. Erskine backed away, shielding his face with his hands. She beat him without mercy, her body trembling, angry in points in her eyes, the whip an extension of her fury. Kincaid watched his daughter and did not speak. Latigo Lansen moved on the ground and held a hand to his shoulder.

It was Hildy Kincaid who helped him to rise. Erskine stood away, face whip-marked, skin tight. Kincaid watched his daughter bend and take hold of Latigo Lansen's good arm. When he stood upright he released himself. "I'll do my own fighting," he said.

"Please . . ." she began. He turned away without speaking, held his shoulder and walked to the horse. In the saddle he looked round. Erskine glared. The woman held fingers to her lips. Kincaid looked from his daughter to the man on the gelding.

"You started it, Kincaid," said Latigo. "When it begins to hurt, remember that."

Kincaid held out a hand to bring him back. "Lansen!" he shouted. Latigo ignored the call. He passed between the longhorn pillars and spurred the horse. She had told the truth. Sunlight shone in his eyes and he didn't know what to think about the bridge. It might never be built.

Erskine picked up his gun and stepped forward, face and eyes angry, chest heaving. "Why'd you do that, Hildy?" he demanded. "Why'd you hit me?"

Her eyes turned cold. "Because you're a coward," she said. "Like everybody else around here. You feel safe when you're on a horse or behind a gun. How many of you does it take to fight only one man?"

Erskine did not understand. His anger was uppermost. "I want to know!" he shouted. "I want to know why you hit me!" He reached out a hand and she moved away from his touch. Kincaid watched the whole thing.

"Don't touch me!" she commanded. "Don't come near me! Don't ever come near me again!"

"What're you talking about?" Erskine shouted. "I want to know what's got into you! Why'd you hit me?"

Kincaid watched his daughter's face. He thought about the man on the horse and the day he had ridden to the Lansen ranch to make a proposition that concerned his daughter. There hadn't been any need for that at the time. Now there was and it couldn't be done.

Erskine's eyes burned. His face paled in rage. "Nobody's making a fool out of me!" he cried. He moved to touch her, to take hold of her arms, to beat sense into her and make her understand that he couldn't be beaten. She stepped away, used the crop and another livid mark wealed on his face.

"Stay away from me," she said.

Kincaid moved. "Joe!" he ordered. Erskine turned, furious. "Go about your work. Leave us."

The foreman stared in sullen anger at the rancher, a long hard look of challenge. Kincaid straightened his shoulders and returned the hateful regard. It lasted for nearly a minute, the woman silent. Erskine backed away.

Her head came up. She had never looked at her father before with the same equality or distance. "Why did you do that, father?" she asked.

"Do what, Hildy?"

"Burn down his house. Ride the boy down . . . shoot him. Why did you do that?"

"Are you sure that I did?"

She was angry. She pointed with the riding crop. "He says so, doesn't he? He recognised you. He heard your voice! Why did you do it?"

Angry woman talking, not his daughter; an angry woman standing up in defence of a man who had been hurt. She had changed completely and suddenly. "I wanted his land," he admitted.

"Why?" she cried. "Why must you own land? What will you do with it?"

"Own it," he said.

"That's not enough, father. You can't own it all. You'll get no comfort from it!"

The thoughts behind her eyes disturbed him. He spoke slowly. "Didn't expect it to bring me any comfort, Hildy," he said. "Wasn't thinking about myself."

Her eyes mocked him. "Don't pretend you were thinking of me, father."

Again he spoke slowly. "Yes, I was," he affirmed. "When you're married to Joe you'll understand what I mean."

Her cheeks flushed red. "No, father!" she said. "Not Joe!"

"He thinks you will."

"He's wrong. He's terribly wrong."

He regarded her calmly. "This is rough country, Hildy," he said. "But women have a place in it . . . beside a man to give him the help he's got to have, and comfort when he needs that. Best of all to give him reasons."

She turned away and clasped the stick of the crop. She spoke without seeing him. "I'm a woman," she said. "I know what's expected of a wife."

"Then you know that women are too scarce to waste," he said. "This is a man's country. It's also the day of the gun, rough justice and hard living. But the rewards are big. It needs strong men and Joe's not strong enough on his own. He needs you."

She faced him again. "It won't be Joe," she stated. "It will be nobody before it's Joe."

The light was on her face. She was beautiful and angry and hurt. He remembered her mother. "Who, then?" he asked deliberately. She didn't answer at once. "Him?" he persisted. "Latigo Lansen?"

She remembered the sound of the gun on Latigo Lansen's forehead and the look that seized his face when his shoulder hit the ground. "Yes," she said in relief and defiance.

Her father didn't fight back as she expected. Instead, he pushed hands down into pants pockets. "Then there's no problem, is there?"

"Yes," she said. "There's a problem. You. The man hates me."

"That's because we're fighting."

"Then stop fighting!"

"I want his land."

"You won't get it, father. He'll fight back. He's got better reasons than you. It's his land . . . it always was his land!"

"You want me to stop fighting him?"

She walked to the verandah steps, halted and looked back. "You better stop fighting, father," she said. "Latigo Lansen is one of the strong men you said were needed here. He'll protect himself. And he means what he says. If this war goes on it will end in one way. You'll be dead or he will. And I don't want him dead!"

"Hildy!" he cried but she had gone.

Kincaid found Joe Erskine saddling his horse. "Joe," he said and waited. Erskine turned from the horse, sullen face whip-marked.

"Yes, Mister Kincaid?"

Kincaid regarded his foreman. Joe was a good man but Joe wasn't part of himself. "We'll forget about Lansen," he said bluntly.

Erskine rested hands on his gunbelt. "What do you mean, Mister Kincaid, forget him? You can't not fight him unless you don't see him and he's there, right on the doorstep."

"I mean we'll leave him alone."

"Why, Mister Kincaid? You started out to run him off same as the others."

"I've changed my mind. Maybe I won't need to run him off."

"On account of her . . . is that it?"

"I'm boss around here," Kincaid said. "I still give the orders."

"Sure, Mister Kincaid, but what about Joe Erskine? What happens to him? I've been made to look a fool and I don't like it."

"This is tough country, Joe. The living is rough. You've got to take things the way they come. I'm telling you now what I want done. Leave Lansen alone."

"Supposing I disagree, Mister Kincaid?"

Kincaid's face became resolute. "Only one answer to that," he said. "You can pick up your money any time you like."

"Just like that?"

"Said it was tough country, Joe. The war is over in Gila river valley. Over and done with. You can go or stay."

Erskine tugged the cinch strap tight and stepped into the saddle. He looked down at the man on the ground. "Whatever you say, Mister Kincaid."

Joe Erskine rode away from the corral rail to look for Latigo Lansen, find him and kill him.

He headed north and stayed on high ground. Lansen would be slow and not covering much territory. He whipped the horse on level ground and reined before he reached the belt of wooded country. He moved lower. He could see the river and hear the sounds of running water. Behind him grazed a thousand cattle. There was no wind to ripple yellow grass. He walked the horse in a trough of land and when he came up on a rise, stood in the stirrups to search and scan.

There was no sign of Lansen, which was as it should be. The man he had hit with the gun couldn't have come this far this soon. He was hurt and would walk the horse, maybe even get down to wet his lips and rest. Erskine rode lower and searched the ground for tracks. When he didn't find any he made for high terrain.

He stayed south of the juniper belt that hid the rocky gash in the earth, a ravine that didn't belong here at all but to wild mountain country; a box-canyon of whitened rock

94

and boulder. Juniper and pinon grew thick and coarse on the high ground surrounding the ravine; inside, scrub clung to rocky soil and cirio wood twisted in sunlight. The place was a natural trap and if Latigo Lansen stayed on low ground, as he should, he would have to ride past the open end, between the canyon mouth and the river.

When he was high Erskine was careful to stay out of sight. He watched the river, the clumps of aspen and willow. He heard a sound that was strange. He looked back and listened. He wished he had brought a rifle.

He saw Latigo Lansen near the river, walking the gelding and not watching high ground as he should have, which meant that the man was a fool. Erskine examined the chamber of his pistol and eased the gun into the holster again. There was plenty of time. He watched the rider down below and allowed him to pass. When Latigo had ridden by Erskine followed, staying high, keeping the other man in sight.

When Latigo Lansen passed out of sight behind the pinon Erskine sprinted higher. At the edge of the wood belt he stepped down and moved on foot into the pinon. The light became broken, the air still. He moved carefully through the belt, came to the edge of the ravine and peered down. Latigo Lansen was just appearing below, not looking up, not aware that he was observed.

Erskine lay down on the ground, raised the gun and sighted from behind his elbow. His forehead and lips sweated and the palms of his hands itched. When the slow-moving figure of Latigo Lansen moved across the gunsight Erskine squeezed the trigger.

The report was loud, filled the ravine and rose skywards. Down below the gelding reared up and the man in the saddle hit the ground. The horse found its feet and cantered, not hurt. Cheek, chin and chest on earth Latigo stared up into the ravine. A figure moved on the upper rim and another shot echoed through the canyon. When dust spurted in the air inches from him Latigo rose knee-high, bent low and ran to the nearest whitened rock boulder. He drew his gun and watched.

On the top rim the figure moved again. Latigo's finger tightened on the trigger. Joe Erskine leaped from the rim, slid to boulder shelter and crouched down. Pebbles slithered on the slopes in sand and dust. Latigo used the gun again and sparks of stone splintered from the rock shielding his enemy. Erskine stood up and fired, clearly seen, the original advantage lost. Latigo recognised the man on the height. He crawled and returned the fire, poised himself on hands and toes and sprang from the boulder. He threw himself into the shadow of man-high rock shelter, clung with palms and chest, leaned out and fired and clung again, safe. Erskine wouldn't get the chance to kill him now.

He thumbed bullets into the Colt. From above he heard sounds, boots on rock and the slithering cascade of descending rubble. For moments there was silence, the air hot and bright. Back and shoulders tight against the rock shelf. He peered along his shoulder, out and up. Whitened rock shimmered in the heat. Another shower of pebbles and Erskine moved. Latigo fired quickly. Erskine whirled and responded. Latigo stood back as bullets bit on stone above his head. He breasted his way from under the overhang.

Using first one foot, then another, testing the ground and finding a good foothold, he eased himself away from the shoulder. He reached a round-faced boulder, spun quickly and used the gun. Erskine saw him move and directed lead. Chips of stone sprang into the air. Latigo crouched and waited. The sound of pistol shots rushed into the enclosure of the ravine, shuddered on rock walls and died away in long swishing blades.

Latigo crawled flat on his belly. He lay behind scrub, Erskine appeared above, on hands and knees, peering down. Latigo squeezed the trigger and rolled. Erskine disappeared. When he returned the fire, bullets ploughed into ground. This was what Latigo wanted. He tossed a rock and a spikey cat-claw bush trembled. Bullets spouted into dust as Erskine fanned the gun at what he thought was the man below. Latigo moved and crept higher, sure that Erskine had lost him. He rolled, crouched, climbed and edged his way up and across the side of the ravine without using the gun again. Instead, he tossed rocks and where a stone landed, Erskine's bullets erupted sand and shale.

Latigo reached the rim of the canyon above Erskine and waited. Minutes passed. The light was strong, the air hot. Light hurt Erskine's eyes and made him sweat. His hands were wet and beads of water formed on his lips. He was imprisoned by the light, the heat, the unknown whereabouts of Latigo Lansen and the passage of time as silent minutes were burned out of existence. When a scrub or cat-claw swayed and a flat stone slithered down out of sight he used the gun blindly, eyes everywhere.

When he knew that he had lost Latigo Lansen, Erskine stopped being careful and clambered back up to the rim of the canyon, scrabbling in haste, rubble avalanching from his heels. When he reached the lip of the ravine and was breathless Latigo straightened from haunches and hit him with the gun.

"That's for the first time you hit me," he said.

Erskine yawed at the edge of the slope. His gun clattered on rubble and slid out of sight. Blood appeared on his face. Latigo stepped closer, swung the pistol and hit him again. "That's for the second time," he said. Erskine went down on his knees, eyes dazed. Latigo stood still nearer and raised the gun. "And this is for now!" he hit him again. A cry escaped Erskine's lips. He fell back from the third pistol blow and lay on his side, knees drawn up.

Latigo holstered the gun. "Go back to Kincaid," he said. "Tell him you should have brought a rifle."

Latigo climbed down the side of the canyon and walked to the horse. In the saddle he looked back to where Joe Erskine writhed on the ground. "Tell him I'm just starting to fight!" he shouted.

CHAPTER EIGHT

LATIGO was buckling his gunbelt when Buck awoke.

"What're you doing, Latigo? Where you going?"

The bunkhouse was shaded but not dark. Outside a round bright moon lit up the sky and made the night clear. Buck rose and stood away from the bunk, face shadowed.

"You going riding, Latigo?"

"Yes."

"At night? It's dark . . ."

"Light enough for what I'll be doing."

Buck watched him spin the chamber of the gun. "Wait, Latigo. I'll put on my pants."

"You're staying here, Buck."

The boy grabbed at his pants. "I'm going with you, Latigo," he said.

"Look, Buck, I'm going to start a . . ."

Buck glanced and nodded. "I know what you're going to do," he said. "It takes two men."

Latigo pushed the gun into the holster. "I'll saddle the horses," he said and went out. Buck came after, tugging the gunbelt tight. He heard the corral rails being lifted down.

The night was clear and calm, only the hiss of the river disturbing the lonely quiet of open places. There was no wind. The horses nickered and then were quiet. Both men mounted silently. Gaunt new roof beams stood out above the blackened walls of the ranch-house like the rib bones of a dead man.

When they reached the water Latigo motioned left and south and they stayed on his side of the river. Moonlight shone on rippling water. Buck looked back to the shadowed ranch-house. Two miles farther on Latigo slowed. "We'll cross here," he said.

Water hissed quietly. Latigo went first and waded the gelding into the river. Buck stayed close behind. Flanks quivered as the animals left the water. Latigo waited for a minute, listening and watching. There was neither sound nor movement.

Buck edged his roan closer. "What range you heading for, Latigo?"

Latigo moved his head. "West," he said.

"How many out there?"

"Three or four thousand."

"You think we'll be able to get them up?"

"We've got guns."

On Kincaid they rode north in a wide round sweep that brought them out behind the western range of grass land. Hooves made a muffled drumbeat on the ground. Far away they heard the bellow of a lonely steer.

They rode for an hour without haste and reined in the shadow of a pinon clump, ground soft and springy underfoot. From cover of the darkness Latigo peered out across the plain, looking east. Night lay reposed upon the range, the air heavy with the scent of pine and saguarro,

98

sage, and mariposa, buffalo grass and cattle, the smell of horses and woodsmoke.

Latigo motioned Buck closer. They had seen no nightrider, no small glow of flame. The pastures were empty save for the resting herds and themselves. Buck leaned across and Latigo pointed. "Out there," he said. "West."

Buck nodded. They left the shadow of the pinon and rode west. In ten minutes Latigo drew rein. They were on the breast of a long wide slope of land. Before them lay the great sweep of valley range, bathed in moonlight and deep in silence. Latigo searched north and south.

"Which way, Latigo?" asked Buck and eased the gun in his holster.

"East," directed Latigo.

"To the house?"

Latigo looked east. "To the house," he repeated. "Right up and in, if they'll go."

Buck wet his lips and settled the gun again. "I'm ready if you are," he said.

Together they moved east, down the slope of land, moonlight making a whim of shadow on the ground ahead of them, hoofbeats deadened by grass. Buck watched as Latigo drew his gun. He slid his own from leather and held it ready.

They topped a rise and looked down. Before and below them spread out the shapeless dark of four thousand head of resting cattle. They walked the horses close and Latigo motioned with the gun. "Keep them going east, Buck," he instructed.

They parted. Latigo waited only minutes. Somewhere in the distance cattle bellowed and calves bleated for the udder. There was no cloud and no wind and the sound of the gun would be loud.

It came as a thunderclap that echoed and snaked out over the heads of slumbering cattle like a whiplash. For moments the air was electric and imprisoned, then erupted in a deep wild rumble. Fear raced like fire through the mass of rising, struggling, bellowing beasts. Lumbering bodies moved and strove. Eyeballs searched the moonlit dark. Nostrils sniffed at crackling air. Latigo used the gun again. The urge became primeval. From half a mile away came answering shots as Buck rode and yelled and shot bullets in the air.

Panic and the sound of panic adding to panic took hold. Latigo reared the gelding and yelled. He fired the gun, lead sent low. A thundering roar climbed up into the sky. Cattle rose and stamped, bellowing. Pistol shots pierced diamond darkness in long arrows of fire. The earth shook.

The great body of cattle exploded in a spreading turmoil of sound and movement, beat the ground in fright and sought escape in headlong eastward flight.

The slope of land became a tide of moving shapes, rushing, thrusting, bellowing, hoofing; an untidy torrent that swept convulsively amain over moonlit ground.

Latigo bent low in the saddle, racing with the charging steers, clear but close. Dust rose in a cloud, beaten from the ground and clinging to the air. Soon the moon was masked, the night murked. He heeled the gelding forward, gun in hand, mouth open, lips yelling till pain rasped his throat. The roar became a mountain of sound that reached skywards. Stamping cattle raced from crowding hooves and biting gunfire. The herd became a shrouded black stain lunging east.

The earth was gouged. What had been yellow grass became a churned-up swathe of broken ground. The dust-spumed sea of bodies moved like a scourge. Cattle rushed headlong.

Latigo rushed with the herd, face coated with risen dust, eyes narrowed. His mind was cold, his actions deliberate and without doubt. When a man goes to war he arms himself with a gun. If he is a savage he takes up a spear. But the best weapon, and the one that hurts most, is that nearest his hand and closest to his enemy. With Kincaid as his enemy Latigo chose Kincaid's own possession, four thousand head of panic-driven beef cattle.

The woman was outside all this. She occupied his mind not at all.

With Buck, it was something different. He copied and repeated everything Latigo did. He yelled hoarsely, brandished and used the Colt pistol and rode with the same purpose. He wasn't afraid. He sat firmly in the saddle, body tingling, in control of himself and the animal under him. He was not aware of courage or misgiving. He had only one regret in his mind; that his father had not done what Latigo was doing.

Together they drove the rushing cattle across the sloping range towards the Kincaid house. The wave of sound reached out ahead of the black tide and swept, with a noise like the rumbling of a cliff face in avalanche, up about the great stone house. When he had used every bullet in his belt Buck holstered the gun and yelled louder than before.

Matthew Kincaid leaped out of bed and ran to the window. A moonlit dust-cloud rose from the western horizon. Thrusting sound beat against window glass. He flung open the window and the noise became thunder. He reached for his gun, fired out into the night and yelled. "Stampede!" he shouted quickly.

His daughter came into the room carrying an oil lamp as he tugged on pants. "Father ... what is it?"

Outside, men shouted and ran and shouted again, racing for horses and saddles and guns.

"Stampede!" cried Kincaid. "Go to your room and stay there! Don't come downstairs. They're headed this way. God knows what will happen!"

Lights appeared downstairs. Men ran to the corral. Horses panicked and circles in dust haze. Saddles were thrown over haunches and cinched. Lights glowed behind windows and from open doors. Matthew Kincaid slung a gunbelt about his waist and ran to the window. "Saddle my horse!" he shouted. "Start a fire out there! Get out there and head them off!" He strode to the bedroom door. "Lansen did this!" he accused angrily. "He's paying me back!"

Her fingers tightened on the lamp. She didn't speak. Radiance clung to her uncombed hair.

Matthew Kincaid stamped as far as the saguarro and shouted. "A fire! A fire!" he commanded.

Bedding was brought and piled high close to the longhorn pillars in front of the house. Men shouted and ran. Horses trumpeted. A wagon was hauled from behind the bunkhouse and overturned, wheels spinning, to make a barrier against which the head of the stampede would crash and crumple. A flaming brand arced in the air and touched the mountain of dry bedding. Coiling smoke billowed, erupted into sudden yellow flame and reached upwards. Darkness fled as the great glow rose and spread. Flame brightened the front of the house and made every window a mirror. Fire mounted, hissing, crackling, biting at air and swirling. Men on foot and on horses became spectres. From the west the roar of stamping hooves stretched from horizon to horizon.

Latigo emptied his Colt pistol and dragged on the rein. The gelding slowed. Stampeding cattle swept past him in a headlong rush. Dust rose high and hung suspended. He watched lights appear in the windows of the Kincaid home and a pyramid of fire rise from the ground.

Buck rode out of the haze close to him, face streaked wtih sweat, voice hurried.

"Let's move, Latigo. We got them up!"

Latigo wheeled the gelding. He and Buck headed north, swung east and made for the river. Neither looked back.

Cattle surged towards the Kincaid house. The ground trembled. Horsemen appeared, riding furiously, using pistols and rifles, making for the head of the stampede, yelling and wheeling close to turn the beasts away from the house, to change the direction of panic flight and bend it north or south to open ground. Some of it was successful but not enough. The herd split and became twin torrents, one headed north to spreading range, the other charging on towards the longhorn pillars before the house.

When it was too late to do more, men scattered and ran for cover. Horses shrilled and beat the ground. Bellowing steers rushed towards the fire. The overturned wagon was lifted high and rode crazily, yawing, standing on end, thrust upwards on the backs and shoulders of plunging, fear-driven steers; engulfed and stamped upon, broken to bits, ripped and splintered and trodden into the ground.

The fire might never have been. A thousand slavering beasts rushed into it and upon it, threshing in smoke, spewing fire into the air, scattering flame, beating it down. Licks and spumes of flame shot up like dismembered hands and fingers to wither and die in darkness. Fire clung to hide and hair; the smell of burned skin became poisonous.

Men with guns in their hands ran for safety. Cattle stormed about the longhorn pillars, crashing like flood water. White-painted corral fences yielded, were broken down, trampled and carried away. The saguarro were flattened and pulped. Horses shrilled as fence rails were whipped into the air. Dust rose in a haze that clouded

102

the sky and hid the moon. The ground shook with the stamp and weight of hooves. Wooden uprights snapped and verandah roof tiles clattered. Dust haze clung to the house.

Hildy Kincaid stood away from the upstairs window, afraid to watch any longer. She heard her father close the polished pine door, the crash of window glass and his voice as he shouted uselessly into the din of roaring, bellowing steers, the creak and twist of breaking wood, the cry of frightened saddle horses, the shouts of men and the crackle of gunfire. The floor beneath her trembled and she clasped the carved oaken bedpost. Her father's voice was hoarse and urgent.

She didn't hate Latigo Lansen. It must have been something like this five nights ago when he had been attacked. There'd been no stamping cattle but there'd been something worse, men on horses armed with malice. That made a difference. This stampede was his way of fighting back. What he had done was only fair.

When the noise and movement outside began to lessen she moved to the window. The verandah was in bits, the steps in splinters. The corral fences lay broken and the horses scattered, the saguarro trodden to a pulpy mess, the ground torn up.

The cattle thinned. Panic died away. Lonely steers stared and bellowed. She heard shouts and voices coming from behind the house where horsemen rounded up wandering exhausted animals. Cattle trotted from before the house and the air began to clear. Voices moved farther and farther away. Hoofbeats faded as steers were driven off. The tumult was over.

Matthew Kincaid entered the room. He didn't speak. She stood by the window, the lamp on a small table, yellow light rich on varnished ceiling and window brocade. Outside, horses rode close and halted. Joe Erskine's voice called out. "Mister Kincaid . . . !"

Kincaid moved to the open window.

"You going after him, Mister Kincaid? You going after Lansen? It was him, all right. Now's the time to do it!"

She waited for her father's reply. He was slow to speak. Horses hoofed restlessly.

"No," announced Kincaid. "There'll be no more riding tonight."

"But, Mister Kincaid, it was him!"

"Put the horses up," ordered the rancher. "Go to bed, all of you. That's an order!"

He lowered the window and straightened. She moved nearer the oaken bedpost. Matthew Kincaid was puzzled.

"It's what you did to him," she said.

"But I'd stopped fighting."

"You didn't tell him."

"I won't crawl!"

"Nobody expects you to crawl. He didn't know the war was over."

He gestured. "It's the size of it," he said. He pointed to the window and what had gone on outside. "He did that himself. All that . . . by himself. That's what I don't understand. He's got Andrew Hemingway's boy with him but he doesn't count. It was Lansen who thought of it and it was Lansen who did it! He did it to me, Matthew Kincaid!"

"Father," she said. "You're only a man. So is he."

He stared at her. "I own the valley!" he shouted. "I'm not a vain man but I'm a big man! I could ride out now and kill him for what he did. And nobody would say I had done wrong!"

"Nobody would say you had done right, either. He's paying you back. He said he would. You started the fight, remember. You can't blame him, father."

His face reddened. "Look out of the window!" he commanded. "Look out there and see what he did. You say I can't blame him for that!"

"You burned down his house," she exclaimed. "You shot him. You gave him a reason and no choice but to come here tonight. He's fighting the way he knows best. He's doing what every other man has the right to do. Live!"

"You want me to admire him?"

"Yes," she said sharply. "I want you to admire him for the man that he is. You say you can't understand how he did all that by himself, but I can. It's so easy to understand that I don't know why you don't. The man's in the right. He doesn't need hired guns. He knows how to fight back, and unless you go to him and make peace, he'll do it again."

"I'll kill him!"

"He said he'd kill you," she reminded. "I believe him."

His face was angry, his eyes puzzled. He stared at her. "Who's side are you on?" he asked.

She stood away from the bedpost. He hair caught the light and was burnished. Her eyes were bright and clear. She reminded him of the woman who was dead. The years had been lonely since then. He repeated the question. "Who's side are you on?"

"I'm on his," she said.

"He hates you," he said.

"Only because my name is Kincaid."

He stared again. "I don't understand."

She did not look away from his troubled face. "I'd rather be a wife than a daughter," she said.

Matthew Kincaid didn't know how far his empire stretched, the number of miles from marker to marker, the thousands of yellow acres, the cattle, horses and men. He'd done it all because he was lonely. Latigo Lansen said it was because he was afraid to die. He was afraid now.

"But I said the war was over!" he shouted.

"You didn't tell him," she said. "He has something to say about when it will end. You'll have to go to him."

"You want to see your father on his knees?"

"No, father, I don't. I want you to ride up to him and hold out your hand."

"I've sat on a horse too long," he said. "My back is stiff!"

She turned away. "That's what you'll have to do, father," she said. The door closed behind her and he was alone.

Matthew Kincaid sat on the bed and clasped his hands. He had not realised before that she was his daughter and that he loved her.

Buck saw the rancher first. They were on the roof placing new timbers and driving nails when the yellow-haired man straightened his long body and held on to the chimney square. "We've got company, Latigo," he said and fingered the handle of his gun.

The rider was still far away, crossing the river to the

Lansen side and disappearing behind aspen that fluttered like imprisoned wild things. "You see who it was?"

"Think it's Kincaid," said Buck. "Maybe we'd better get down."

They were on the ground when Kincaid appeared. Latigo reached for the rifle and jacked a bullet into place.

"You going to kill him, Latigo?"

"Maybe. If he starts anything."

They stepped forward and waited. Kincaid's sorrel moved slowly up the draw and approached where they stood. Buck stayed yards behind Latigo and rested a hand on gunhandle. The walking horse halted. Kincaid clasped hands about the saddle horn and looked down. "I'm not armed, Lansen," he said. "Came here to talk."

"Go ahead. Talk."

"Don't aim to talk sitting on a horse. Don't aim to get down unless I'm invited."

Buck's hand moved away from his gun.

"You can get down," Latigo said to Kincaid.

The landowner stepped down stiffly, regarded the two men before him and nodded slowly to Buck. Defeat wasn't alone in having the taste of ashes; years did, too. The yellow-haired boy must be all of six feet tall, and well shaped. They made a good pair, he and Lansen, for there wasn't a whit of difference, except that it was Lansen's land and Lansen who made the decisions. The rancher's eyes narrowed on Latigo Lansen's tall spare frame.

"You know what it's like to take a man's life away from him?"

Buck clasped hands on his gunbelt.

Latigo shook his head. "I've killed men," he said. "Don't know how they felt. I was doing it to save my own life so when it was done I was glad to be living."

Kincaid looked back to his own land on the other side of the river. "All that land," he said. "All my cattle . . . my house . . . the years I've lived here . . . everything."

"I didn't take them away from you," Latigo said.

"They're not worth having," said Kincaid. "The price is too high."

Buck's long body eased. He listened. Latigo lowered the rifle and held the gun across his thighs. "Don't know what you mean."

Kincaid's head came up. "Came to talk peace with you,

Lansen," he said strongly. "Not because I want to but because I have to. Sometimes life deals a real unexpected card."

"Never played cards. I'll talk peace."

"I'm not crawling, Lansen. I didn't come here to beg. I'm a bigger man than you. I'm richer than you. I can run you off this land any time I want."

Latigo raised his rifle to his shoulder. "And I could kill you right now," he said.

"Latigo!" said Buck. Latigo lowered the gun. Kincaid nodded.

"The boy's got good sense, Lansen," said the rancher and filled his lungs. "Fact is, I'm not only fighting you. There's somebody else as well."

"Nobody I know. There's Buck and me. That's all."

"There's my daughter," said Kincaid.

Buck turned away, walked to the corral and stood by the rail. He saw but did not hear any more.

"What's she got to do with it?" Latigo asked, but only to give himself time to think.

"Reckoned you'd know, Lansen," said the rancher. "I can't go on fighting you because she's on your side. I can afford to lose my land, my cattle and my money. Can't afford to lose my girl."

"She say that?"

"She said it."

That was it, then. The bridge was built, the water would run clear and sweet and he'd be able to ride his horse over pine logs. Buck stood away from the fence and watched. He knew something good had happened.

"All right," said Latigo. "I'll make a peace with you."

Kincaid held out his hand. Buck stared as Latigo accepted the rancher's clasp. "One thing you've got to understand, Lansen," said the older man. "I'm not a coward. I'm not hiding behind my daughter. You hurt and surprised me last night but that I can take. That's the kind of fighting I understand. You don't frighten me but you win because of her. I reckon we'll always be enemies, you and I."

"I didn't come here to be anybody's enemy. You started the war."

"Maybe. A man makes his life the way he thinks it should be done. Some get hurt."

"You hurt yourself, Kincaid," said Latigo.

Kincaid climbed back into the saddle. He reflected. "Maybe I did," he admitted. "You're welcome at my house, Lansen."

"Thanks. I'll wait a while."

"What for?"

"Figure to let the water clear a bit first."

"Whatever you say. Hear you're bringing in new stock."

"Waiting every day for word."

"How many?"

"Two thousand three hundred. The three hundred are for Buck."

Buck heard his name mentioned but not what else was said. He didn't try to listen.

"That's fair," said Kincaid. " 'Day, Lansen."

When the rancher had gone Latigo laid aside the rifle and stuck thumbs into his gunbelt. He regarded Buck for a whole minute without speaking. Buck did not look away. Latigo shrugged. "Come on, Buck. We've got to get this roof on."

Buck tossed a four pound hammer into the air and caught it again with a swing when it came down. Neither of them said anything about what had happened.

CHAPTER NINE

REBECCA NEVIN brought the news. Buck leaped from the roof to be first near her and ran to the horse. She allowed herself to be helped down. Buck beamed and felt as big as ten men. Latigo walked from behind the house.

"Latigo! This here's Rebecca!"

"Howdy, ma'am."

"This is Latigo, Rebecca," said Buck.

"I brought a message, Mister Lansen," she said. Buck led her from the horse. "Your cattle are coming in tomorrow. Ed Harrison asked me to ride out and let you know. He said it was very important that I bring the message."

Latigo grinned. "Yes, ma'am."

Buck flung his hat in the air, leaned back and yelled.

"Yippeeee!" he cried. Rebecca held fingers to her ears.

Latigo grimaced. "Last time we got word like that," he said. "Buck and I wrestled. Guess it wouldn't be fitting to break his back a second time."

"Latigo!" shouted Buck.

"Did the message say what direction they'd come from?"

"The trail boss sent a rider on ahead. He's in town now. Reckons the herd will reach north of town by tomorrow noon. They'll wait till you come. Mister Harrison said you were to ride into town now and talk to the messenger."

"Buck can do that," said Latigo. "Get on your horse, Buck. Ride back with Rebecca and talk to the messenger."

"Yes, sir!"

Buck made ready and mounted. Latigo looked up. "We'll need some help, Buck. Do what you can."

"If I see anybody in town I'll hire them for the day. Reckon we could do it ourselves, anyway."

"Don't want to take any chances. Try and get help."

"Sure, Latigo. Come on, Rebecca . . ."

Latigo stood alone then. He walked to the circle of white stones and touched the Indian lance with his hand. Tomorrow he'd have stock on his range. In a month his house would be ready to live in and there'd be a woman in it, waiting for him to come home.

He walked north of the house to where there was a rise of land. The sun stood high in the sky and a wind sang in the grass. The air tasted fresh and clean, without heat. He stood for a long time in the open.

In the morning Buck was too excited to eat. He had the horses saddled and ready and came rushing back before Latigo had finished his second cup.

"Hurry up, Latigo! You going to drink coffee all day?"

They rode north across open valley range, the air warm, the sky empty. They skirted the twist in the river and moved through a pinon-filled hollow. Behind them the mountains rose high and sharp and free of haze. Cactus clumps, fantastic and spiked, were gaunt and beautiful native poetry.

When they approached a rise, and there was a different scent in the air, Buck rode ahead. He reined on the rise, waved and shouted back. "Latigo!" he yelled. "Latigo!

They're here!" Latigo rode alongside. Buck's face shone. He pointed. "That's something, eh, Latigo?"

The cattle lay resting. A haze of dust hung in the far distance. Steers bellowed and grazed on yellow grass. Buck watched his partner's face and waited for him to speak. There were no words.

They moved down the hill and a man on a horse came riding forward to meet them. "Trail boss?" asked Latigo.

"The name's Murphy. You Mister Lansen?"

"That's him, all right," answered Buck.

"Your cattle, Mister Lansen. We lost a few head on the way. Nothing to make any difference."

"Did you have a hard time?"

"No. Was easy. Nice herd of stock you bought yourself."

"You'll be coming into town with us?"

"Thanks, Mister Lansen. Like to accept your hospitality but I haven't got the time. I'm leaving right now. Sent my crew back an hour ago, soon as we got here. I'm going on to Tucson. Got to pick up another bunch."

"Thanks. We'll take them from here." Latigo held out his hand and Murphy returned the grip.

"Good luck with your cattle!"

In minutes the lean-faced man was out of sight and Latigo and Buck were in charge of two thousand three hundred head of cattle. Buck stared lovingly at the browsing herd. "They sure look pretty, Latigo," he said. "They're so pretty I could get down off my horse this minute and stroke them. Guess you're glad."

Latigo nodded. "Some of them are yours," he said. "You should be glad, too."

"I'm sure glad, all right. What do you want done, Latigo?"

"Want them moved, Buck. Where's the help you said was coming?"

Buck stretched in the saddle and looked behind. "Be here any minute, Mister Lansen!" he said. "Be right up!" Latigo turned. Three riders trampled grass and rode alongside; Ben Nevin, Ed Harrison and Rebecca. Latigo stared. Buck grinned widely.

"Figured you'd need a little help," said Ben Nevin.

Latigo swiped a long arm with a wide-brimmed hat at

110

the end of it. Buck laughed and leant away. "What about your store?" Latigo asked Harrison.

The big man shrugged. "Figured the best way of safe-guarding the money you owe me was to help get these cattle home," he said lightly. "They look nice. Do you proud, Latigo."

"Right," said Latigo. "Buck and I will stay at the tail end. Ben Nevin and Ed Harrison will side-trail east and west. Rebecca, you ride along with Buck."

They did it with shouts and the flat crack of whiplash. The herd lumbered, was slow and noisy at first, then began to move. For such a big man Harrison was quick and lively on a horse and his cattle cry was as loud and commanding as Buck's. Nevin rode to the west and kept the herd from rising ground. The cattle were in good shape, fat and sleek of hide; dusty but not tired. Movement was easy.

Buck's shoulders heaved as he swung the long whip and cried out. "Yi . . . ! Yi . . . ! Che! Che! Hiiii . . . ! Yip, yip, yip!" Rebecca rode close enough to watch his face and catch his glance when he sought her eye. The voice that came from a full chest was loud and strong. The sun was high and a great swathe of trampled grass marked the passage of the cattle across the range.

Latigo rounded up wandering strays. The lash of his whip snaked out and smote the air. The sound of the moving cattle became the sharp hiss of breaking grass, slower than the rush of river water, but louder.

At the end of an hour Buck swung away in dust to ride alongside Latigo. "You figured on a brand yet, Latigo?"

It was long moments before Latigo answered. He wanted to enjoy what he had to say. "Sure," he said slowly, almost in reproach. "Figured a long time ago."

"What's it going to be, Latigo?"

" 'LB'," said Latigo and kept his face serious.

Buck leaped in the saddle. "Yippeeee!" he shouted. "Yarrupp!" and rode to tell Rebecca before the wonder died.

The herd moved over short grass like the shadow of a cloud against the sun. Ben Nevin cried "Hiyaah! Hiyaah!" and kept the high ground clear. Ed Harrison divided his time between leading and herding. They slowed in the cactus beds and skirted pinon belts.

In early afternoon Ben Nevin rode back to find Latigo.

Ahead of them lay the twist of the river and it was time to rest. He rode alongside and wiped his face. "Been thinking, Latigo," he said. "Any reason why we can't take them across the river? Save hours going round."

"You mean the twist?"

"Yes. Wouldn't matter much if we crossed the river twice. Going round that loop might keep up out till dark."

"Inside the loop is Kincaid's land."

"The war's over, isn't it?"

"Wouldn't do it without asking."

"What say you do that? We'll hold them here before they start smelling water. You go see Kincaid."

"Right. Tell Buck what I'm doing."

He rode ahead and splashed across the river. When he looked back the herd was out of sight. On the opposite bank he turned south and headed for the Kincaid house. After two miles he reined and waited for the approaching riders to come abreast. Matthew Kincaid sat stiff-bodied and erect. The woman's hair was tied in a plaited bun and uncovered. Her eyes met Latigo's in a long straight look. He touched his hat and she smiled. " 'Day ma'am,'' he said. " 'Day, Mister Kincaid."

The rancher watched them both. He clasped the saddle horn and regarded Latigo Lansen. "For people that are taken with each other," he observed. "I'd say you were formal."

Latigo nodded. "I said I'd let the water clear."

She watched his face as he spoke.

"So you did," agreed Kincaid. "Hildy and I thought we'd ride out and see your cattle come in."

"Glad to have you. It's why I'm on your land. Like to ask something."

"Go ahead."

"Two or three miles back the river loops. Going all the way around will take hours and more, maybe keep us out till dark. Wanted to know if you'd let me bring the herd across your land."

"No reason why not. Sure, Lansen. Go ahead. You can't afford to waste time."

"Thanks," said Latigo. He touched his hat to the woman. "Nice to see you, ma'am." He wheeled the gelding.

"Wait," said Kincaid. "I'll ride with you. You might

112

need some help." The rancher addressed his daughter. "You coming or staying, Hildy?"

"Till you've crossed the river," she said. "I have things to do back at the house."

"So you have," nodded Kincaid and glanced at Latigo. "Don't forget, father."

"I won't."

She watched them ride away and was glad when one of them looked back. Kincaid was a yard in front and did not see Latigo turn in the saddle. He made no sign other than to turn. He noted that she no longer carried the riding whip.

Miles from her Latigo and the rancher reined at the loop in the river. "Here, you mean?"

"Better than going miles round."

"Sure. Crazy river to twist there, anyway."

They splashed in water and went on. On the range Buck rode forward to meet them, surprised at the presence of Kincaid but saying nothing. "All right to go on, Latigo?"

"Sure thing, Buck. Start them moving."

Buck swung the stockwhip. "Hiyaah! Hiyaah! Che ... ! Che ... !" he cried and the cattle moved, bellowing.

Kincaid and Latigo rode to the side of the strung-out herd. "See you got help," said the rancher. Ben Nevin rode by in dust and swung his hat.

"Yah! Yah! Yah!"

"Ben Nevin and Ed Harrison," said Latigo. "Friends of mine."

Kincaid eyed the slim figure of Rebecca riding close to Buck. "And the girl? She your friend, too?"

"Buck's the man you want to ask about her."

"He's Hemingway's boy."

"That's right. Buck's my partner. Some of these cattle are his."

"What happened to his folks?"

"They went north."

Kincaid headed the sorrel south. "I'll lead," he said.

The cattle smelt water. Kincaid led them to the river. The herd moved on a wide front down into water and drank. Rebecca walked her horse to where Buck, dusty-faced, straight-backed, waited, resting in the saddle. "Things sure have changed around here," he said when she was close. "Kincaid himself helping out."

"Some of the cattle are yours, Buck," she said and thought him the handsomest man alive.

"Yes, ma'am," he said. "Three hundred of them belong to me. Never knew a man like Latigo in my whole life. You know anybody else in the world who'd give you three hundred steers?"

Latigo waved a hand. "Hiyaaah!" shouted Buck and swung the whip. Rebecca backed away from him. The cattle moved across the river and on to the other bank, Kincaid leading, Nevin and Harrison side-trailing and Latigo and Buck driving from behind. The river swirled away muddy and dark.

Then over the rising ground of the loop and the long slope down to water again. It took an hour. Hildy Kincaid watched as the dark mass of cattle swelled over the crest of the hill and trot smoothly and quickly on falling ground, bellowing and puzzled by a second breadth of water. Her heart beat faster when she saw her father out in front, riding like a young man, heard the cries of the men on either side and then saw Latigo Lansen and Buck come into sight at the tail end of the herd, riding in dust and not clearly seen. She envied the dark girl who rode some distance behind the two men, closer to one than the other, and who looked, from this far away, like Rebecca Nevin.

When the press of beasts had crossed the river and were rising to the Lansen bank she turned away. Joe Erskine, who had also watched the leading cattle churn water, followed. She heard hoofbeats, reined and looked back. A wind flowed over yellow grass. Erskine rode alongside and halted. She wondered where he had been and why he had come. There were bruise marks on his face and temple. "Father's down with the new stock," she said.

He nodded. "Saw him there. It's you I want to talk to."

"Later, Joe."

"Now, Hildy. All I want to do is talk."

The difference between the two men was simple. It should have been evident a long time ago, as far back as the moment she had first set eyes on Latigo Lansen.

"You going to marry me, Hildy?" he asked.

She moved her head. "No, Joe. That's over. I'm sorry if you're hurt, but it's over."

They were alone on the range, the herd of cattle and

114

the men in charge of it out of sight and out of hearing, but she wasn't afraid.

"Is it him?" Erskine asked. "Down there by the river . . . is it Lansen?"

"Yes," she said. He didn't move and he didn't seem either surprised or hurt. He didn't smile and his eyes remained distant. He shrugged as though it didn't matter.

"You might be sorry, Hildy. A man doesn't like being made to look a fool."

"I'm sorry, Joe," she repeated. "That's the way it is."

"In that case I reckon it's time I was heading in another direction."

"That would be the thing to do, Joe," she agreed.

He squinted in the light, face creased, the look different. "Just hitch up my pants, ride away and be forgotten? Is that what you mean, Hildy?" She didn't answer him. Depth returned to his eyes. "Yeh," he said to himself, not to her. "Yeh . . ."

She heeled the horse and left. He watched her out of sight and rode to where he could see the last of the cattle wading from the river on to Lansen land. He heard the shouts of the men and the sounds of the whips, being used for the last time and then coiled. He turned and rode west.

As the last steer left the water and stood sniffing grass on Lansen land Buck waved his hat. "Yeeeeoooooh!" he yelled. "They're home!"

Kincaid left the head of the herd and rode back to Latigo. The cattle began to spread out and wander, free to graze and settle down. "Getting late," said the rancher. "How far you taking them?"

Ben Nevin and Ed Harrison also rode close and it was Nevin who answered Kincaid's question. "Reckon they'll do where they are, Latigo," he said. "They'll wander some before they settle down, but that's all right. They're still on your land."

"Anyway, they're home," added Harrison. "Nice looking beasts."

Latigo agreed. "Reckon we'll call it a day," he said. He shouted to Buck. "What about you, Buck? Ready to quit?"

Buck was tired, his belly gnawing. "If I don't eat soon, Latigo, I'll die! You figure to let them stay where they are?"

"They'll move around a bit before they settle. We'll look at them tomorrow."

Kincaid wiped his forehead. "You've got a nice herd of cattle, Lansen."

"Thanks for helping me bring them in," said Latigo. "You, too, Ben and Ed. Couldn't have done it otherwise."

Harrison shrugged lightly. "No trouble, Latigo," he grinned. "Just protecting my interests, that's all."

Latigo laughed. "You're a liar, and you know it!"

The big storekeeper was pleased. "Maybe," he admitted. "Reckon we'd best be heading back to town, Ben."

Buck looked quickly at Rebecca. Every minute of the day had been the better for her presence. She didn't speak. Kincaid did. "Hildy said I was to bring you back to supper, Lansen," announced the rancher.

But there were good hours to be spent out among the scattered cattle, looking at them, feeling proud of them, feeling right about everything. "Don't think I'd better, Mister Kincaid," he said. "Buck and I have things to do."

"She especially said I was to bring you."

"Go ahead, Latigo," urged Buck. "There's nothing to be done I can't do. The stock won't need watching."

"You've got to eat, Buck, and you can't cook!"

The silence lasted for moments only. "I'll make Buck's supper," said Rebecca. Buck looked sideways. So it wasn't over yet. There'd be hours to spend after sundown, standing by the river near the willow, watching the sky burn, rushing from day into night. This was even better than the day he had brought the first news of the cattle coming.

"There's no roof on the house yet," he said quickly. "Latigo and I live in the bunkhouse. It's not cleaned up or anything."

Ben Nevin moved his horse. "Let's go, Ed," he said to the storekeeper. "See that she gets home safe, Buck."

"Yes, sir. I'll do that."

Harrison and Nevin moved away. Latigo climbed on the gelding ready to go. Kincaid regarded Buck Hemingway. "How old are you, boy?"

Buck looked away from Rebecca, his face straight. "I'm eighteen years old," he said.

Kincaid's regard did not waver. "I guess you hate me," he said. Buck did not answer. Rebecca Nevin moved closer to her yellow-headed man and he was aware of her pres-

116

ence. "Reckon you think I did wrong, driving your folks off their land."

"You did wrong," said Buck. "Everybody knows you did wrong."

Kincaid stepped into the saddle, his gaze intent. "Why didn't you fight back, boy? The land was yours."

Buck's look sharpened. "Not because I was afraid of you," he said. "Until Latigo came I didn't know how."

Kincaid moved the sorrel. "Didn't say you were a coward, boy," he said. "Anyway, nothing's been done that can't be undone. Let's go, Lansen."

"Won't be long, Buck," said Latigo.

Later on Buck stood by the Indian lance that pierced the ground out in front of the burned ranch-house. Valley-scented air fanned his face. He heard the hiss and gurgle of Gila river water. He breathed and turned to find Rebecca by his side. "What do you think Kincaid meant when he said that?" he asked.

"It sounded good, Buck," she encouraged. "I think he meant your father could have his land back again."

He nodded sharply, hopefully. "That's what I wanted it to be but I was scared to think it." He hitched his gunbelt. "What're you going to cook, Rebecca? We've got some refritos from yesterday and there's a side of bacon. I sure like frijoles fried a second time."

"That's what it'll be, then."

"Come on . . . I'll show you."

It was late when the first shots echoed out through the calm darkness. Gunfire beat the night with the sounds of whips. Latigo was rising to go. He straightened and listened. Kincaid sat upright in his chair, cigar in mouth, forehead creased. Hildy Kincaid looked quickly towards the window. For seconds, until the third and fourth shots sounded, all three remained motionless. The gunfire was distant but clear, some of it from a rifle barrel.

Buck Hemingway stood with his shoulders against a tree trunk that was cool to the skin under his shirt. Rebecca Nevin sat on a low rock boulder with her hands clasped. The air was clear and bright with moonlight and until now the only sounds had been the swish of river water. Buck leaped from the shadow of the tree and listened. The gunfire came from the north. "It's on this side of the river!" he

117

said. When the third and fourth shots sounded he ran for his horse. "Something's up!" he shouted. Rebecca ran behind. By the time he had the saddle cinched a rumbling noise was rising into the air. He straddled the roan. "Stay here, Rebecca!" he ordered. "Don't move away from here! Do what I tell you!"

She watched his dust rise into moonlight. She called his name. "Buck!"

Latigo flung open the polished pinewood door of the Kincaid house. The shots had come from his side of the river. Now there was the rumble of hooves, far away but plain. He reached for the gunbelt as Kincaid rose from the chair.

"What is it?"

Latigo tugged the buckle tight. "You know what it is, Kincaid," he said. "It's a stampede!"

"Latigo . . . no!" she cried.

Kincaid jerked upright. "Now, listen here, Lansen . . . !"

Latigo reached the door again. He turned. "I should have killed you when I had the chance, Kincaid!" he said.

"You're wrong, Lansen! I didn't . . . !"

"Latigo . . . please!" she cried.

"You knew this would happen," Latigo said, eyes on the startled rancher.

"I had nothing to do with it, Lansen!" Kincaid shouted.

"You don't have to be there personally! Joe Erskine does it all!"

He ran to the gelding and Hildy Kincaid followed, reaching out a hand to hold him back, to make him listen. "Latigo! Latigo . . . please!"

Kincaid came running. "Lansen, you're wrong!"

Latigo stepped into the saddle and swung the gelding. "Where's Erskine?" he demanded. Kincaid was confused. He pointed to the bunkhouse.

"There . . . over there. He'll be in the bunkhouse!"

"Get him!"

Kincaid shouted. "Joe! Joe Erskine . . . ! Erskine!"

The door of the bunkhouse opened and a cowhand stood in the patch of yellow lamplight. "Something you want, Mister Kincaid?"

"I want Jot Erskine! Where's Joe Erskine?"

The man shrugged. "He's not here, Mister Kincaid.

118

Been away for an hour or more. Took two men with him ... said you had something for him to do."

Latigo glared down from the saddle. "Who's lying, Kincaid?" he demanded.

"I didn't!" shouted Kincaid in white-hot anger. "Damn you, Lansen, I had nothing to do with it!"

"I don't believe you, Kincaid," said Latigo. "The war's on again! If anything happens to Buck, I'll kill you! You hear? I'll kill you with my hands!"

He drove in his heels and the gelding raced. From the north the rumble of stampede rolled loud and clear. Kincaid stared after him, angry and insulted. The cowhand waited in the lighted doorway.

"It was Joe," Hildy Kincaid said quietly. "Joe Erskine did it."

Kincaid stared at her. "You mean he did this on his own?"

She inclined her head. "It was because of me."

"What do you mean, because of you?"

"I said I wouldn't marry him."

"When?"

"Today ... out near the river, when the cattle were coming in."

Kincaid shouted again. "Get the men out!" he commanded. "Get my horse! Quick!"

Men came running. Kincaid turned and strode towards the house. She followed. "Father ..."

"I'm going after him!" shouted the rancher. "I'll find Joe Erskine and I'll kill him! I'm boss around here! Hurry up, you men! Get over to Lansen ground and break up that stampede. Get our cattle away from the river!"

Buck raced north, clear moonlight above, a rising rope of dust hanging behind, and somewhere on the northern range the rumbling swish of stamping hooves. A dangerous thought exploded in his mind. The stampede couldn't be broken up or halted by himself alone but the cattle might be led. If he could swing the leaders round in any kind of circle they'd slow down. He might split the herd and lead some away. They had to be kept clear of the river.

When he came in sight of the rushing body of cattle he tugged on the rein and drew up, frightened for seconds by the dark horde of thrusting steers. The earth trembled and a haze of dust rose to hide the moon. He looked back and was alone. He dug heels into the roan's flanks and rode ahead.

With space between himself and the first charging cattle he drew his gun and fired straight into the dusty mass of rushing steers. Two stamping beasts fell to the ground and were churned to blood and earth. A third and a fourth collapsed and were trodden into the ground. His horse shied up. He clung with knees and thighs and swung east, ahead of the stampede and clearly in sight. The cattle split and a narrow river of running steers followed his dust. He hoped that Latigo would come.

Latigo raced away from between the longhorn pillars of the Kincaid house and headed east to the river. To the north the air swelled with the roar of cattle and the crackle of gunfire. He thought of Buck Hemingway; one thought only and reaching no further than the yellow-headed man's face. Buck Hemingway.

He swept over rising ground, moonlight bright, skirted a pinon belt and reached a higher level. Noise of the stampede rushed about him. He beat the horse and whitened water ran from his chin as the gelding stamped on moonlit river water. On his own land he turned north and kept clear of aspen and willow. He saw a light in his own rofless house and Rebecca Nevin running out to meet him. He didn't stop. She waved an arm and pointed north. "Buck!" she cried.

Latigo heard her voice only once before she was left behind. From his own high ground he saw the climbing dust cloud. He thrust with his heels. The gelding convulsed under him. He raced on. Ahead of him another rider dashed through swirling haze, facing the stampede and using a gun.

"Buck!" yelled Latigo, his voice stamped into the ground in the beat of hooves. "Buck!"

Buck Hemingway's roan reared up, pawing in fright, eyes wild, tail in the air, and swung east when rowels cut across flanks. A long snake of cattle followed blindly.

As the breakaway sloughed past, Latigo repeated the tactic. He used the gun and three lumbering steers were ground into the dust. He swung east and cattle followed his lead. He raced after the yellow-headed man in front. There was no longer any light, the air thick with haze, heavy with rushing sound. "Buck!" he yelled. "Buck ... where are you?"

The rider he had seen disappeared, swallowed by dusty darkness. Frenzied cattle stamped on his voice.

Joe Erskine levelled the rifle and squeezed the trigger in alarm and rage. A bullet sliced the noisy air. A shrouded figure rode past followed by a narrow breakaway stream of slavering steers. Erskine twisted in the saddle, face streaked, and raised the gun. Dust belched about him and hid the other horseman. He squeezed the trigger and didn't know if he had killed the rider or not. The stream of cattle thundered on. He swung his horse and raced after the main body of cattle. Two horsemen rushed out of clinging dust before him. He pointed and yelled.

"The river! The river! Get them into the river!"

He clung with knees to the saddle and held the rifle high. Bullets whipped the air and shuddered. The men at his side used pistols. The sound of guns flattened to hovering sheets. Cattle leaped and rushed.

"Kill anybody you see!" yelled Erskine. "Head them for the river!"

Haze climbed steadily into the sky.

Matthew Kincaid came rushing from the house buckling a gunbelt about his waist. "Come on! Come on!" he shouted. "Get going! Get it broken up right away! You hear?"

Six riders heeled horses and raced away. When he reached his own he turned and pointed a hand at her. "Now you get in the house and stay there!" he ordered. "This thing's going to be cleared up once and for all! You hear me, Hildy? Stay in the house!"

She heard and did not speak. He stepped into the saddle in temper and haste and swung off into moonlight. Dust followed him between the stone pillars and where the saguarro had grown. When he had gone she saddled a horse.

Kincaid rode north on his own land, skirted the pinon belt, followed the river, swung east to avoid the rocky canyon, then north again. From then on he kept close to the river. The sound of the stampede rolled out to meet him and he found his jaws tight with wrath and determination. If Lansen's crazy cattle were near the river they'd have to be driven back. His own cattle would rise if they smelt any of the panic that was driving Lansen's steers wild.

He stamped through water and rode on sloping Lansen land. The noise swelled loud and close. He heard gunfire. When he topped rising ground and could see the horizon of dust he found the stampede moving south, parallel to the river but not close enough to be in danger.

Kincaid rode west and close and side-trailed, used his pistol and shouted. He heard six-gun and rifle fire from behind and could see nothing. He beat the sorrel forward, calculated what his position ought to be, and edged to the head of the stampede. Bellowing steers swung away as he approached. He yelled and used his gun. One after another four charging steers crashed to the ground and were stamped to hide and hair. The leaders began to swing east.

Latigo galloped out of dust. Kincaid shouted. "Get behind me!" he cried and brandished the gun. "East!" he yelled. "Keep them east!" Latigo rode ahead of the rancher, closer than Kincaid. "Get back!" yelled the rancher. "Get back, you crazy fool!"

Latigo paid no heed. He rode close and used the Colt. Fear drove charging steers away from the gelding's crowding hooves. Slowly the head of the stampede turned east in a great whorling circle.

The gelding stumbled and went down on forelegs in dust, reins, crest, tail, hooves and saddle trappings. Latigo crashed to the ground. Kincaid hauled on the halter and swung aside savagely, the sorrel rearing. He looked back. Dust rose in twisting coils. All he saw was a movement of black on the ground as Latigo Lansen rolled and rose and ran. Cattle splayed past. The gelding raced away, lost and shrill.

Buck Hemingway hoofed into sight ahead of the rancher, face sweating and streaked. Kincaid shouted and pointed back. Buck stared behind as he hauled on the rein. "Lansen's down!" shouted the rancher. "Back there! Go for him, boy!"

The roan pranced as Buck leaned to the side and dragged on reins. He whipped the horse and headed back. In seconds and within yards Latigo's gelding loomed greyly, pawing the air, eyes wide, crest wild. Buck swung his long body low and grabbed at trailing leather. The gelding backed and shied up, shrilling. Buck wound rein

122

thong about wrist and was harsh. The gelding came in tow. "Latigo!" he shouted. "Latigo!" He circled in dust, searching and crying out.

"Here, Buck! Here . . . !"

Latigo rushed out of the swirl, shouting and waving his arms. Buck saw the shrouded figure and raced both roan and gelding. Dust rose in a mist as Latigo reached for the saddle horn and leaped astride the gelding in one continuous movement.

"They're moving east!" Buck shouted. Latigo shoved with his heels and rode ahead. Kincaid looked back as the two men came up behind.

"Keep them east!" shouted the rancher.

Latigo swung out into the lead, Buck followed to second place and Kincaid fell back to third. They rode single file, close to the cattle, forcing the leading steers away from the river.

Kincaid eased and slowed his sorrel. Two of his own men rode alongside. He pointed with the gun. "Stay with Lansen!" he shouted. "Keep them turning!"

Joe Erskine watched the movement of cattle become a whirlpool, with strings of beasts, lost and confused, straggling on the edges of the sworl. Up front somebody had beaten and crowded the herd away from the river. He yelled and brandished the rifle in the air. "The river!" he cried. "Get them into the river!"

His riders hauled on reins and wheeled east to side-trail to the head of the stampede and bend the leaders back towards the west. Erskine stayed where he was.

As the movement continued east and became a wide spreading circle, Erskine came closer to Kincaid, who had slowed. Moonlit dust hung heavy and thick and all that could be seen was the dark mass of moving cattle, shrouded. and confused, turned inwards upon itself and eventually to lose force and thrust. Erskine didn't know what was ahead of him and Kincaid, who was searching for his foreman, didn't know he was riding to meet him and that in minutes they would clash.

The herd was turning when the two men rushed at each other. Erskine rode from the haze, saw the rancher's stocky figure on a horse that had leaped forward out of nowhere, and hauled on his rein. The horse reared with a loud shrill cry. Kincaid heard. Erskine hung low in the saddle, rammed heels to flank and swung away. Kincaid recognised the head and shoulders of his foreman, reached for his gun and shouted.

"Erskine!" he yelled angrily.

Joe Erskine rode through rising dust with the rancher following. Kincaid leaned forward in the saddle and squeezed the trigger of the pistol. The shadowy figure ahead of him veered in haze and darkness and the bullet went wide. The rancher fired again and shouted.

Erskine, surprised by the presence of Kincaid, confused as to the reason and angry because of it, made a sudden and irrevocable decision. He remembered the words Lansen had spoken when confronted by Kincaid and six other men on horseback, and he remembered also the discovery he, himself, had made at that moment. Everybody dies. He intended to kill Lansen later on when the cattle had been driven into the river, but here was Kincaid.

Erskine dragged the horse to a halt, levelled the rifle against his shoulder and waited. When the shouting, angry rancher was within yards of him he squeezed the trigger. The report was loud. Kincaid's body slumped and his shoulders came forward to help press out the terrible pain that filled his chest. His head sagged low and his hands lost hold. The noise of the stampede raced away from him in a long receding needle. Suddenly there was no light in his eyes. He died on the horse as the pistol slid from his fingers.

Latigo and Buck Hemingway came abreast of the cattleman as he swayed and rolled from the saddle. Buck's feet touched ground first. Latigo drew on the rein. "Get him up, Buck!"

Buck was on his knees. He stared up. "Latigo! He's dead!"

Latigo dragged the gelding round. He shouted down. "There are men behind you. Get off the ground, Buck! They're heading this way! Get off the ground!"

Kincaid's men leaped down. Latigo went on. He heard Buck's shouting voice behind him. "Latigo! If it was Erskine, I've got debts to pay! Latigo . . . !" Latigo raced on.

The herd had turned full circle, would trample the same ground a second time, tightening, soon to become a hard,

124

tightly-packed mass of bodies unable to move. A rifle bullet whined past Latigo's shoulder. He hung low. Ahead of him a horseman careered through dusty darkness. Latigo beat the gelding forward, came close enough to recognise the sweating face of Erskine and drew his gun. He shouted as Erskine's horse went down in a threshing crash. The foreman rolled clear and slung the rifle to his shoulder. Latigo was on top of him, ready to leap from the saddle when Erskine squeezed the trigger. Latigo dragged on the rein. The bullet went wide. The noise of stamping hooves rushed close. Dust swirled between man and man. "Erskine!" he yelled. "Joe Erskine!"

When the rushing cattle were a hundred yards from him, thrusting darkly from the blanket of haze, and Erskine on foot somewhere in the middle of it all, Latigo swung the gelding about. He heard one long loud strangled and penetrating human cry above the noise of stampeding steers; drawn-out, hoarse and then stamped to silence. He holstered the gun, rode away from the sound and did not look back. When he came to where Kincaid had fallen from the saddle there was no sign of the rancher, or of Buck. He rode on.

Kincaid's men controlled the stampede. Panic died quickly. Without the sound of shouts and guns the cattle calmed and what had been a swelling whirlpool of sweat-streaked animals became a great pressed-in mass of air-sniffing bodies. Noise drained away. The haze of dust returned to the ground. The sky became bright again with clear moonlight. In an hour it was all over. Quiet drifted over the range. Cattle that were no longer imprisoned or driven by fear broke up slowly and wandered, lay down to rest. Soon the river could be heard.

Hildy Kincaid rode to where Latigo stood. Men stood near, not speaking. When she stepped down from her horse they scattered and left only Latigo. She knelt but she did not weep. When she looked up, Latigo spoke. "Erskine," he said. "It was Joe Erskine killed him." She did not look away. "Erskine's dead, too," he said.

Kincaid was raised onto his saddle. Nobody spoke. Latigo rode to the Kincaid house, the woman by his side, Buck Hemingway, coming from another direction, saw what was happening and walked his horse back towards the river. In front of the Kincaid home, with light shining from windows and the open pinewood door, she stepped down. The Mexican manservant came forward, clasped his hands and bent his head. She was calm when she spoke, her voice quiet. "He's dead," she said. "That clears the water for ever."

"It's clear," said Latigo. He moved towards the gelding and her hand touched his arm.

"I don't want you to go," she said.

He left the horse and walked indoors.

In the morning while the light was still cool he saddled the gelding to go home. She came to the door of the house and watched. "Latigo, I want to ride with you," she said.

He helped her mount. Out on the plain, in sight of the river, a wind crossed her forehead and combed her hair.

"We've got a lot to talk about," Latigo said. "All this land."

"The future?"

"Yes, ma'am."

Buck came riding out to where Latigo and the woman sat on horses. All at once the yellow-haired boy was a man, tall and with a man's hands on the reins. "Ma'am," he said. "Yesterday your father said some things to me. He didn't exactly say it in words but the idea I got was that he was willing to sell us back our land. Does that still go?"

She glanced at Latigo but his eyes did not tell her what to do. "Yes, Buck," she said. "That still goes."

"Thanks, ma'am. Is it all right if I ride north and find my folks, Latigo?"

"Where's Rebecca?"

"She's home. I slept there last night."

"Get going, Buck," said Latigo. "And hurry back. You've got cattle to look after."

"Yes, sir. 'Day, ma'am. See you, Latigo."

Latigo and the woman watched Buck ride down the long slope of yellow-grassed land and head north. When he was out of sight and they could no longer hear the hoofbeats of the roan, Latigo turned. "When Buck comes back, ma'am," he said. "Don't sell him the land. Give it to him."

"Yes, Latigo," she said. "Whatever you say." She petted the long silky neck of her horse. "The bridge is built," she said. "Couldn't you walk across it? Couldn't you call me Hildy?"

"Yes, ma'am," he said and looked at the sky. "I'll call you that from now on."